Fouling Out

GREGORY WALTERS

ORCA BOOK PUBLISHERS

Library and Archives Canada Cataloguing in Publication

Walters, Gregory, 1964-
Fouling out / written by Gregory Walters.

ISBN 978-1-55143-714-9

I. Title.
PS8645.A49F68 2008   jC813'.6   C2007-907385-9

First published in the United States, 2008

Library of Congress Control Number: 2007942401

Summary: Faced with the realities of his friend Tom's home life, Craig must determine the boundaries of their volatile friendship.

Orca Book Publishers gratefully acknowledges the support for its publishing programs provided by the following agencies: the Government of Canada through the Book Publishing Industry Development Program and the Canada Council for the Arts, and the Province of British Columbia through the BC Arts Council and the Book Publishing Tax Credit.

Cover and text design by Teresa Bubela
Cover artwork by Margaret Lee
Author photo by West Coast Photo

ORCA BOOK PUBLISHERS
PO Box 5626, STN. B
VICTORIA, BC CANADA
V8R 6S4

ORCA BOOK PUBLISHERS
PO Box 468
CUSTER, WA USA
98240-0468

www.orcabook.com
Printed and bound in Canada.

11 10 09 08 • 4 3 2 1

For Doug, wherever he may be.

Acknowledgments

I am grateful to my editor, Sarah Harvey, for patiently helping streamline my words. Less is more!

I must also thank my dogs, Lincoln and Hoover. They are the ones that sacrificed the most. More than anything, they provided me with plenty of distractions when I simply needed to enjoy the moment.

One

Nothing much happens when you're twelve. Too young to work, too young to run in the Olympics, too young to drop out of school. Of course, being "too young" has its advantages. I don't have to go to work, and I don't have to listen to oldies radio stations.

The bad part is that you can really get in a rut at my age. With school at the center of everything, I don't see how it can be any different. At least there's summer to look forward to, but that's not much of a consolation in October.

I suppose anyone can be in a rut at any age. In fact, when you think about it, most people live pretty routine lives, but either they don't even notice it or they don't want to call attention to it. Nobody wants to admit he leads a dull predictable life, but I was never good at pretending. Being Craig Trilosky is a mundane existence. My teacher, Miss Chang, would kick up a big fuss over how great it is that I used the word *mundane*. She gets all excited about really dumb things. Unless you're a brain who gets straight As, school's just a place where teachers get to point out all the things you can't do. Miss Chang's not really like that, but it's still early in the school year. She'll end up being like the others. She may have noble intentions, but she's got Tom and me to shatter all that. There isn't a teacher on the planet who wouldn't crack.

You can't get any more mundane than my family. I don't think there could be a more boring group of people on Earth. My dad's an executive for a big electronics company in Vancouver. I don't know his exact title. It changes every month or so—manager, senior manager, vice president of this, vice president of that. I bet there's even a vice president of job title creations. I don't see why we have to "celebrate" each of his promotions. It never increases the amount of my allowance.

Mom's a professional volunteer. She works with Meals on Wheels, the Red Cross, the Easter Seals Society, AIDS Vancouver and the hospital. She used to be a nurse. I once asked her why she didn't quit all the volunteering and take a paying job with some worthy cause, and she acted all hurt. Add that to the unwritten list of things that cannot be discussed in the Trilosky household.

I guess it's okay that she does that stuff. I just hate Thursday afternoons. That's when she volunteers at my school. Usually she's helping in the library, which is all right because I never go there, but sometimes she's in the halls putting up notices on the bulletin boards or walking with some kindergartener. She has no idea how embarrassing it is having her at school. When my class sees her on the way to PE, everyone sings out, "Hi, Mrs. Trilosky," just to make me turn red. She thinks they're being friendly.

My sister, Margo, is in grade eleven. She says it's pretty hard and there's a lot of homework. (I think someone forgot to tell Miss Chang that she's teaching grade seven, not grade eleven.) Anyway, my sister's all right. We used to fight all the time, but now she's preoccupied with talking on the phone and text messaging. She's got her own cell phone because my dad has fits about needing the landline for business calls, even though he's got a cell phone and a Blackberry. I think talking on the phone's boring and kinda gross. How do you know the person you're talking to isn't going to the bathroom in the middle of the call?

My sister's on the track team at school; I run with her on Tuesdays, Thursdays and Saturdays. Sometimes I do a solo run on Sundays. It's actually a lot of fun. You don't have to depend on anyone else and you don't have to worry about letting your team down. I like that part best. When it's just me, I'm fine. The group stuff never seems to work out.

I don't really have a lot of friends at school. I spend too much time hanging out with Tom Hanrahan. When we moved here five years ago from Toronto, he was the first one to welcome me and ask if I wanted to play soccer after school. We've had a lot of good times, but he always gets me into big trouble. The vice principal, Mr. Skye, gets to see me at least once a week, and you should see the look on Mrs. Neuman's face every time I walk by the library. It's like she thinks I'm going to take a geography book and shelve it in the sports section. I'd go in and do it just to tee her off, but she's so old I'm afraid she'd have a heart attack.

I'm tired of everyone thinking Tom and I are a team. Most parents around here have forbidden their kids to have anything to do with Tom. The Hanrahans are the source of endless gossip. People say Mrs. Hanrahan is a weak woman who can't control her kids. Mr. Hanrahan showed up drunk at last year's Christmas concert, and he was arrested a couple of years ago for getting in a fight with a police officer. Tom's sister is supposedly deep into drugs, and he has two brothers, but no one has seen the oldest brother in years. The rumors about him are wild— most have something to do with prison. My parents don't like me hanging out with Tom, but I can't seem to connect with anyone else. I want to hang out with other guys, but nobody will have anything to do with me because nobody likes Tom. I'm finally starting to feel that way too. I definitely need to get out of my rut.

Two

On the soggy soccer field at McKenna Park, Tom squishes a couple of wet worms and curses the fact that there are no slugs to be found.

"Hey...who do you think I should go for?" he says. "Erin Patterson or Tracey Lin?"

Why is he asking me for advice? Don't they have to like you first? I stare off at a parked car to avoid eye contact. "I don't know."

"Well, Erin's cool 'cuz she's tall and good at basketball and she knows players' names and all, but Tracey's got a real good smile. I mean, she must be the only girl in seventh grade who doesn't have braces. Her teeth are perfect."

How can I argue with that? I've never examined Tracey's teeth. I've never even thought about who wears braces.

"Well, c'mon, stupid." Tom flings a moist worm from a small stick and watches it sail several meters. "Who should I go for?"

"Whoever you like best." I sure hope the worms are already dead. They certainly aren't meant to fly.

"What kind of lame answer is that? I like them both so just tell me...Erin or Tracey?"

"If I pick one of them, that would be it? That's who you'd go after?"

"Sure."

"I think you should make up your own mind."

"Stop trying to weasel your way out of it." Tom crouches close to the ground, searching for his next victim. "You're my friend so you have to decide."

A man and his bouncy beagle approach the parked car. Oh, please, save me! I need a getaway! "I don't want to decide. I don't like either of them."

"Don'tcha see? That's perfect! That means you're not biased. If you liked one of them, you'd tell me to go for the other one so you could have the one you liked."

"Who says you get who you want?"

"Well...*you* can't, but I can get either of them. Girls like me. I just gotta take my pick."

Wow! What planet is he living on? Where is he getting his information? All the girls think Tom is loud, disgusting and annoying. Come to think of it, that's what everyone in school thinks—boy or girl. And I'm beginning to think they're onto something.

"Hurry up! Stop all your stupid thinking and just pick for me. You're my friend, so you have to."

"Who says? Where'd that come from?"

"From me!" Tom barks, sounding as exasperated as I feel. He zooms in on another worm, scoops it with the stick and lets it fly. Maybe I should start a Save the Worms campaign.

"Well, what happens if I don't pick for you? Then what?" He continues to stir up dirt, but comes up wormless. Maybe worms have some kind of high-frequency warning system we can't hear. Maybe now the torture will stop—at least for the worms.

"You have to pick or I'll beat you up."

"Yeah, right. After you supposedly beat me up, do I still have to decide for you?"

"Yep."

"That's crazy."

"Pick. Tracey or Erin." Tom drops the stick at his feet, giving up the hunt. I wish he'd give up on this girl-hunting thing too—or at least leave me out of it. I'm feeling like a hunting dog responsible for bringing some pitiful dead duck to his master. Hey, I think I just compared girls to ducks. Obviously, I've got my own dating dilemmas.

"Didn't you hear me?" Tom shouts. "I told you to pick. Does Erin get to have me or is it gonna be Tracey?"

That's it. I'm tired of his nonsense. I don't care. I want to move on and talk about something else before the whole Saturday afternoon gets away from me.

"Fine, I'll pick. Eenie meanie miney moe. Erin."

"Really? Why not Tracey?"

"You're kidding, right?"

"No." Tom picks up a rock and scans the sky. Great. He's moving on to targetting birds. Yep, this is the guy all the girls want. Poor Erin. I really don't have anything against her. Tom stops gazing at the sky and continues his interrogation. "Why'd you say Erin instead of Tracey?"

"I don't know. You told me to pick one, so I did."

"Yeah, but now you have to explain it."

"No, I don't. You said you'd go after whichever one I picked. I picked and that's that." Tom searches the sky again. I really don't want any bird to fly within target range, but it'd be a nice surprise if one somehow manages to poop on his head. He's got it coming.

"You can't just pick and not explain. What's wrong with Tracey?"

Quick. Make up a flaw and get it over with.

"She's too giggly."

"I like her laugh. She laughs at things I say."

"No. She just laughs at you. It's nothing personal. She laughs at everyone and everything. Like I said, too giggly."

Tom throws the rock into empty sky. Thank God for short attention spans. He looks straight at me again. I can see he hasn't given up the stupid girl thing. "Tracey Lin's got a nice giggle."

"Whatever. Go after her then."

"I can't. You picked Erin."

"Yep, I did. Too bad. Decision's final." I get up and start walking across the park. Sometimes no one's gonna save you. Sometimes you have to save yourself.

"What about Taryn McCloskey?" Tom calls out, rushing up behind me, smacking his basketball from hand to hand. "Should I go for Erin or Taryn?"

At this moment, I feel like even the flying worms are luckier than me.

Three

A couple of minutes before dismissal, everyone scrambles to gather all their homework materials while Miss Chang talks above the din, instructing us to fill out our planners, and recapping her advice about tonight's assignments. There's no time to groan about her unreasonable expectations or to interrupt her and attempt to renegotiate the load. The countdown to freedom is on.

It is always a race out the door, and Tom always wins. I have to be at least Top Five or he greets me outside with a punch to the shoulder and some griping about how I'm blowing his whole afternoon.

Where is my writing notebook? How can something I'd been using only an hour ago sink to the bottom of my desk? I pull out a dozen things before it surfaces. Out of the corner of my eye, I sense Tom glaring at me. As I stuff everything else back in my desk, the bell rings.

"Tom, Craig...I need to see you." Miss Chang's voice is loud enough that there's no way to pretend we haven't heard. Tom lets out a huge sigh and drops his backpack so everyone else has to dodge the unexpected addition to the obstacle course.

"Let's get this over with," he mutters, passing me and approaching her desk. As I follow, my brain replays the day's events and tries to figure out where I committed a noticeable offence.

"It's your math tests," she begins. "Your scores are rather low."

Tom laughs. "Well, duh. Check your files. We're not real brains."

Miss Chang doesn't snap at Tom about showing some respect. Instead she says, "I know you can both do better. I think if we go over the concepts for a few days after school, you'll—"

Tom yelps. "You gotta be kidding! You want me to do *more* math? On my own time? Why don't you just cut off a couple of my fingers?"

Miss Chang's forehead creases, but she doesn't flinch. "I really think—"

"Do we hafta stay?"

"No, but—"

"We're outta here. C'mon, Craig."

For the first time in my life, I think about how a teacher feels. I guess I always knew teachers had feelings, but the only ones I ever notice are pretty basic.

"Mr. Osmond's mad." "Miss Ogilvy was really nice today." "Wow! Is Skye ever grumpy!"

Miss Chang had offered to give me a second chance. She thinks I'm capable of doing better. She's even willing to give up a chunk of her after-school time to help me.

And I walked out.

I can't blame Tom. Sure, he did all the talking and he decided to walk out, but I didn't have to follow. Why did Miss Chang talk to us together? If it had been just me, I'd have stayed.

Does she really believe I can do better? Or was it just a con job to get me to do more work? I've *never* done well in math—not even on a single math test. Maybe I should tell her. Why should she beat her head against a wall? I've taken dozens of math tests in my life. She's only graded one of mine so far.

Still, if Miss Chang thinks I can do better, maybe I can.

The world looks different at six in the morning. Quiet and still. Had I really set my alarm that early? I always get these wild ideas late at night about what I'm going to do the next day. Come morning, I dismiss my plans with a quick, "Ha! Who are you kidding?!"

Getting up an hour earlier than usual is crazy. I somehow manage to turn off the alarm and then drift in and out of a not very restful doze.

As I toss and turn, I smash my elbow against the headboard. If there's a funny bone in there, it doesn't have an early morning sense of humor.

The pain requires me to sit up in bed and gingerly hold my wounded arm. Stupid headboard. Who was the idiot who invented such a ridiculous piece of furniture? If it hadn't been there…Okay, the wall would've been just as bad.

There's nothing more annoying than losing an argument with yourself.

Still in pain and thoroughly disgusted, I get out of bed and head for the shower. 6:23 AM. I must be crazy!

I arrive at school at 7:58, an hour before the start of classes. The halls are empty except for a couple of teachers casually chatting about some TV show. They almost sound like normal people. It's absolutely creepy.

I startle Miss Chang when I walk into the classroom. She's already writing directions on the board.

"Craig! Have you checked your watch today?" Miss Chang asks. She sounds far too cheery.

"I was wondering if you could help me in math."

Without hesitation, she moves to a clean part of the board and begins writing a fraction problem. Oh, God. No! What was I thinking?!

"You did well, Craig," she quietly tells me at recess a few days later.

"Really?" I ask. What kind of joke is she trying to play? I look in her eyes, trying to get to the truth.

"You worked hard for this. I'm very proud of you." Wow! She's one hundred percent sincere.

As Miss Chang shows me the retest, I see another percentage. I got a B. Not a high B, but still a B. I've never done so well on a math test in my life. I'm stunned.

"Go enjoy the rest of your recess," she whispers, pulling me out of my stupor. I shoot Miss Chang a big goofy grin. It goes against the code of never letting anyone see I care about anything in school—other than PE and maybe Computers. I must look positively dorky, but Miss Chang politely holds back any urge to laugh. She flashes me a satisfied smile. I want to walk nonchalantly out the door, but my feet overpower my mind, and I dance away in an awkward skip-jig. If she wasn't laughing before, she probably is now.

Tom is already involved in an intense game of basketball by the time I arrive at the court. He doesn't know I took the retest or that I've been going in early for extra help. I'd told him to walk to school with Erin in the mornings to try to get to know her better. He liked that idea. Without a doubt, he'll make fun of me if he finds out what I'm doing. I still want to tell him about my grade. I want to tell someone—anyone.

Maybe when I get home, my parents will take me out to celebrate the same way we do for Dad's promotions. Then I remember that Dad's in Seattle on business. It doesn't matter. I couldn't be happier.

Four

There's nothing worse than rain on Saturday. Except for rain on Saturday and Sunday. Unfortunately, it rains a lot in Richmond. A little drizzle isn't a big deal, but this is one of those times when each cloud seems like a sponge that will never wring dry. I was stuck grocery shopping, plant shopping, card shopping and just plain aimless shopping with my mom all day Saturday. The promise of a Big Mac didn't help.

I have to make sure that Sunday won't be a repeat performance. Mom and Dad have a big day planned, choosing paint for the living room. Sample strips cover the coffee table, and their current favorites—named after tasty desserts and exotic vacation spots— are taped to the wall above the sofa. This will be one of those tedious, month-long projects that my parents bond over.

Thankfully, Tom answers the phone when I make my getaway call. He whispers, so I know his dad is still asleep. Sometimes on weekends Mr. Hanrahan sleeps until three or four in the afternoon. Tom once told me that it was because his father liked to play pool and get drunk most nights. Actually, Tom didn't need to say a thing because I'd figured it out. You've never seen such a scary sight as Mr. Hanrahan when he wakes up. Foulmouthed, reeking of booze and cigarette smoke, his hair—what's left of it—shooting out every which way.

Anyway, we agree that I should go to his place to hang out even though we can't figure out what to do. Tom refuses to come to my house because my mom is around; she and Tom barely tolerate each other. She says he's a bad influence and she blames him for all my visits to the school office. Dad, on the other hand, pins the blame fully on me. No excuses, no justifications.

When I get to Tom's, we try our best to talk in whispers, knowing it'll be bad news if Mr. Hanrahan gets an early awakening. No one else is around, which is pretty typical. Mrs. Hanrahan practically lives at her church. According to Tom, she doesn't go there to volunteer. She goes to pray. I'm sure she has a long list of things to talk to God about. Tom's older brother, Jerry, is working at an office supply store. He's the shining star of the family because he made it halfway through eleventh grade before quitting school. (One time when Mr. Hanrahan was in a good mood, he bragged, "We Hanrahans are smart. We all finish school early." Tom said it was his dad's idea of a joke.) Tom never knows if his sister is home or not. She's taken over the basement, which is where we used to hang out. Now the door is always locked. As far as I know, she doesn't work. Mostly, she stays downstairs and smokes pot. No one seems to care.

For the first little while, things go fine at Tom's. With nothing to do, we raid the kitchen. Pickings are slim, but we create some really bizarre sandwiches. I have to eat what Tom makes and he has to eat what I make. (After a lot of arguing, we agree that dog food can't be included.) His sandwich has mustard, beets, fruit cocktail and tuna. I make one stuffed with horseradish, yogurt, oatmeal and lima beans. I gag a little on the tuna sandwich but manage to get a mouthful down. Tom spits out his first bite of the lima bean special, and it sprays all over the counter. I don't let him off that easy, so he has to take another stab at it. We take the leftovers outside, and his dog, Archie, finishes them off. Except for the beets.

We're in the living room flipping channels on the TV when Mr. Hanrahan comes barrelling in, swearing up a storm. As he approaches Tom, he throws an ashtray at him. It misses Tom and takes a small chunk out of the wall. Mr. Hanrahan yells some stuff about "shuttin' up, cleanin' up, and learnin' manners" as he yanks Tom off the sofa and starts kicking him.

I don't even know what I shout out, but I just want Mr. Hanrahan to stop. For a moment, he lunges toward me, but then he turns back to his son as Tom tries to roll away. Tom yells at me to get out of the house, which is exactly what I do.

I've never been more ashamed of myself after I walk—
or run—home. I keep thinking about what I should've
done, what I could've said. Why had I gone over there?
I knew Mr. Hanrahan was sleeping. Would Mr. Hanrahan
have punched me? Maybe I should've run to a neighbor's
to ask for help or call 911. Now that I'm gone, what will Mr
Hanrahan do to Tom?

I nervously wait for my parents to come home.
As I wait, I think back on all the times I've seen Tom's
dad go berserk. Lots of yelling and swearing about
how useless Tom and the rest of the family are. Once
he even started to yell at me—something about my red
T-shirt set him off—but Tom quickly grabbed me and
we took off to play basketball. He broke a beer bottle on
the floor once. Mostly he threw things at walls. But I'd
never seen him get physical with Tom before. Maybe
he's been trying to be on his best behavior with a guest
in the house.

I go over and over in my head how to tell my parents
what happened. I don't have any idea how they will react.
Sure, Mom will forbid me to go over there again, but I
don't know what my father will do. I grow more anxious
as I sit in the living room, jumping up every time I catch
a glimpse of a car in the street.

I want to call Tom to make sure he's okay, but I'm
afraid of what he'll say and of what might happen if
Mr. Hanrahan is the one who picks up the phone. Maybe
just the sound of the phone will set him off again.

When my parents get home, I don't have the guts to say anything. Mom is busy holding up swatches against the living room furniture, and Dad is back to reading his business magazines. I want to throw up, and it has nothing to do with fruit cocktail and tuna. I feel like the worst friend and the biggest coward who ever lived.

On Monday, Tom is at school at the regular time. He looks no different than usual, aside from the fact he's wearing jeans instead of his regular basketball shorts. He doesn't mention anything about the day before, and neither do I. There are certain things about Tom that aren't up for discussion. I don't recall how or when I figured that out, but it was clearly understood.

Five

It's Saturday morning, and I'm staring at a bowl of soggy Shreddies. My mother still insists on pouring the milk the moment she hollers for me to come down for breakfast. It's cereal! What's the rush? The mushy mess puts me in a foul mood, so I start complaining about how I have to spend the weekend reading a whole novel and then writing a paper on how the story would change if I added a famous person as a character.

Totally unreasonable assignment, right? Good parents are supposed to say something like, "Oh, you poor thing" and tell you they're going to talk to the teacher. My mom cuts me off with, "Oh, it'll be fun!" And Dad just tries to out-whine me. "You've got it good, Craig. Just wait till you get a job. It's Saturday, and I'm off to a meeting." Yeah, I think, as he grabs his brief-case and heads for the door. He's off to a buffet breakfast at a fancy hotel in Vancouver. Life's rough when you've got to talk a little business while you gorge yourself with waffles, omelettes and a separate plate loaded with bacon. Besides, he picked his job. Nobody gave me a choice about school.

I go up to my room to mope. The moping gets interrupted when I fall asleep. I wake up and it's afternoon. Study time is over. I decide to spend the rest of the day playing the new Space Explorers computer game in my dad's office, but the doorbell rings before I'm even halfway to Jupiter. Dad's off running an errand before flying to Calgary on business, Mom's out setting up for an evening benefit for one of her causes—kids with leukemia or an endangered owl habitat—and my sister is working on a school project at a friend's house. That leaves me to get up and get rid of whoever's interrupting my space mission.

Tom. We haven't been hanging out as much since I saw his dad beat him up. The time apart hasn't been such a bad thing. I get in an extra run during the week and I've been messing around on the computer whenever I put off or finish the heaps of homework Miss Chang assigns. Really, there hasn't been much time for friends.

"Hurry up and close the door," Tom says as he lets himself in. "Look what I got." He fishes around in his backpack and pulls out a gun and points it straight at me, his eyes bugged out and his mouth twisted into a demonic grin.

"What the hell? Don't point that at me."

"Scared ya, eh?" Tom laughs and shoves the gun back in his pack. "I ain't gonna waste a bullet on you, so relax, man. We're goin' huntin'!"

I'd feel safer going with Elmer Fudd. "Forget it. You're crazy. I'm busy."

"Ah, come on. I just want to kill a squirrel and cut it open. Check out its guts. See if I can cut fast enough to catch the last couple heartbeats. It'll be fun!"

"I'm playing a computer game," I say. "I'm in the middle of a mission that'll get me beyond our galaxy if I'm successful." I head back upstairs, but Tom follows me. I wish there was a way of transporting myself for real.

"Don't be such a geek. Computer game? Space? Are you nuts? It's Saturday, man. Let's shoot some squirrels."

Are you nuts? He actually asked if I was nuts. Wow. I may enjoy pretending I'm an astronaut, but he's the one who needs the reality check. I stare at the computer screen and hope he'll get bored really fast and take off. Out of the corner of my eye, I see him toss the backpack on the floor by my Dad's bookcase. He flings himself sideways into the leather armchair.

"How long's your stupid mission gonna take? It gets dark at, like, four nowadays."

"Could take all afternoon. It's a pretty sophisticated program." As I try to focus on the screen, Tom lets out heavy sighs at a steady rate of three per minute. At one point he burps and then spends a couple of minutes laughing.

"You could play too," I say, figuring his fascination with his own belches will wane and he'll want to talk about hunting season again.

"It's Saturday. I don't do computers on weekends. Quit being a nerd."

"It's really pretty cool. Just give it a try."

"Do you get to kill anything?"

"No."

"What's the scariest monster in it?"

"It doesn't have monsters. It teaches you about—"

Shows, explains, demonstrates. There had to be fifty words I could have used other than *teaches*. He pounces all over it and won't let up. "Teaches?! Nobody's teaching me nothing on my time off." Half an hour later, we're heading to the park on a hunting expedition.

"Let's just play some basketball. Nobody'll be at the court at school."

"Gotta be honest with you, Craig. I'm kinda bored shooting hoops with you. Even your layup is lame. You got no skills. For a while, it was amusing, but now it's not even worth making fun of."

Sure, he could be more tactful, but I couldn't argue. Basketball is okay, but it's not my thing. Back when it was Bump and 21, I could play along all right. My dribbling was fine, my passing competent, but I just never managed to put everything together. I only brought up the sport to distract him from the hunt, but Tom wasn't taking the bait. Pretty amazing since his brain is at least ninety-five percent basketball. In his own mind, he's been in training to go pro since midway through grade two. On top of that, the guy can name every player in the NBA, spout off up-to-date stats for the season and give a solid analysis to explain any team's loss or win. Over the years, I've grown skilled at avoiding any buzz words—swish, Magic, foul—that might trigger a long-winded b-ball lecture. If Tom could dribble the ball in class, he might absorb a bit of school stuff too. The rest of us wouldn't learn, but that's the thing. There's Tom and then there's everybody else.

"Look, I can tell you're freaked out over this gun thing. We'll kill one squirrel and that'll be it. We don't have much time before my dad's shift is done anyway." Tom tosses the backpack on the ground just as we get to the woods. Not much of a woods really. Just a clump of trees between a bunch of houses and the high school field.

"You know," I say, "we could look on the Internet and find a demo of a pig dissection or something." Tom is examining the gun close up, turning it from side to side, waving the firing end every which way. I don't know where to stand.

"Nice try," Tom mutters after a few seconds. "You're not getting me back in front of a computer. We already did your thing. It's my turn now." Tom gets up and walks farther into the trees. "Let's go. Keep quiet and let me know when you see one. This place is loaded with 'em."

Loaded.

"What are you doing back there?" Tom asks as he looks at me over his shoulder. "Are you doing some *Run away, little squirrel* dance?"

"That's an idea—"

"Quiet. There's one up in that tree on the left. Don't move." Tom holds the gun in the air and points it at the squirrel, which is now motionless on a branch, willing us away. Poor thing has a patch of fur missing near its rear. For some reason, that gets to me.

Before Tom pulls the trigger, I jump on his shoulders and knock him down. In mid-tackle the gun goes off. The distinct sound of broken glass follows.

We both swear at the same time, out of pure shock. Where was the glass? What broke? Did someone scream? Is anyone hurt?

Tom spits a couple times as he shoves me off and gets to his feet. "What the hell'd you do that for? Are you stupid?" Okay, tackling Tom as he was about to fire a gun was stupid, but I'm not about to admit that to Tom. He started the stupidity—by bringing along a gun and wanting to shoot it; I just expanded it. Tom scans the dirt in search of the gun, which he must've dropped during the scuffle.

"What'd you hit? Did you hear glass breaking?" I ask.

"What did *I* hit? Obviously not a freakin' squirrel. You messed it up." He spots the gun a few feet away and hurriedly puts it in his backpack as he looks around to see if anyone has shown up to investigate the noise. His crazed hunting smile has vanished, and I can tell he's as close to total panic as I am. We both crouch down and hide behind a couple of trees and peek at the closest house, which is just beyond the nearby fence.

The bullet has cracked an upper window. I swear under my breath as I slide against the tree and sit down hard on the ground. Tom keeps staring at the point of impact. I keep swearing as cold sweat floods my forehead and underarms.

"Hey!" Tom whispers. Is that excitement in his voice? Is he a psychopath? A psychopath with a gun? "Isn't that Robert Montgomery's house? Yeah, I'm sure it is!"

I get up and take another peek, still keeping my body hidden by the tree. Tom's right. I'd been to Robert's a couple of times. The dormers and the orange trim are pretty distinctive.

"Don't you get it? We're cool! The house is empty. Robert moved months ago," Tom says.

"There was a moving van there a week ago. They were moving a bunch of stuff in," I reply. My voice shakes as I start to comprehend what has happened. "Oh, God! What if you killed someone?!"

"Me? You did it. You knocked me down. I only wanted a squirrel. It's all your fault."

"I told you all along to forget about the gun, but you—"

"Never mind. Let's get out of here and get the gun back in my dad's closet." He shoves his face about three inches from mine. "No one's gonna find out about this," he hisses. "Right?"

Six

As I'm waiting in Tom's backyard for him to ditch the gun, every scene from every cop show I've ever watched flashes before my eyes: slamming the criminal against the side of the squad car and handcuffing him, shining bright lights in the guy's face down at the police station, screaming at him until he confesses, tossing him into solitary, escorting him down the corridor in Death Row to the electric chair...Clearly, we're toast.

Where's Tom? How long can it take? What if he's taken off out the front door and left me to face the swarm of cop cars all alone?

Finally, he comes back out and sits on the back steps. I walk over to join him. For once, he looks scared. Archie sits beside Tom and licks his face. Tom seems to be hugging the dog more than petting him.

I wait for Tom to speak. "You don't think we killed someone, do you?"

"I don't know." What else can I say? We'd run from the scene—a crushing piece of evidence when the jury decides between life imprisonment and The Chair.

"Even if the bullet hit somebody, it probably wouldn't kill them. A shot to the arm isn't too serious."

"No," I agree, not wanting to argue the point.

"Unless we hit a baby."

He isn't trying to freak me out. He's serious. He is pale and it looks like he might cry. He hugs Archie tightly, and the dog licks his hand. What happened is starting to sink in. I try to think of something sane, something reassuring to say, but my brain has shut down while my body is going crazy: my feet tap frantically and streams of sweat drizzle from my forehead, upper lip and underarms. It's all I can do not to whimper or bawl. Sitting around isn't helping. "We need to go over there and see if everything's all right."

Tom nods his head repeatedly. I half expect him to call me an idiot and tell me it's a crazy idea, but he just keeps nodding. Finally, he speaks. "Here's what we do. We walk over there from Thompson Road. I'll carry my basketball, so it'll look like we're gonna shoot some hoops at the high school. If there's no car in the driveway, then chances are everything's okay. We'll watch the news tonight. They always report shootings, so if anything bad happened, we'll know for sure."

Tom gets up and grabs his basketball from under the steps. He doesn't look at me to see what I think of the plan, and I have no intention of raising any what-ifs.

We don't say anything as we walk. I keep imagining police scenes while Tom bounces the basketball. It isn't his normal dribbling. It's more like a trance sort of thing.

As we turn off Thompson Road, I see exactly what I don't want to see. Not only is there a car in the driveway, but there's also a police cruiser parked in the street; small groups of people stand on the sidewalk and on nearby lawns.

Tom stops bouncing the ball. I start seeing television and movie scenes again. The cops throw me facedown onto the pavement while the mob chants "Killer, killer!" and tosses whatever trash they can find—empty soda cans, used Kleenexes—at me. Okay, I've *definitely* watched too many police shows. I make a pledge to myself to stick to sitcoms and cartoons from now on. I want to run, but my legs keep dragging me toward the crime scene. Still, our pace has slowed considerably.

"We have to stay calm," Tom whispers. "Just stay calm."

We are now four houses away. There are no police officers outside the house. They're probably inside, investigating the scene, tracing the corpse with chalk. After that, they'll photograph the bloodstains on the walls and pull some carpet fibers. Funny, there isn't any yellow tape surrounding the property yet. I spot Gwen Ledder, one of my sister's friends, on the sidewalk across the street. I tell Tom she can fill us in.

We try to look casual as we cross the road. From out of nowhere, Tom passes me the ball. Of course, it hits my shoulder and drops to the ground. Tom and I glare at each other as I pick up the ball and pass it back.

"What's going on, Gwen?" I ask as we approach her.

For a moment, she doesn't seem to recognize me. Then it registers and she says, "Someone took a shot at the new family's house. A bullet went right through a back window."

"You're kidding!" I respond, trying to earn my Oscar. "Are they okay?"

"Oh, yeah. It just broke a window. No one was in the room. They're pretty shaken up though. The woman was screaming and crying on the front lawn until the police arrived. My mom went over and tried to comfort her."

"Did they catch who did it?" Tom interjects.

"No. They think it's a hate crime. The family's Chinese, and someone spray-painted their garage door last week too. It said something like *Float Home*. Pretty sick, eh? My dad helped them paint over it the day it happened."

"Yeah. Really stupid," I say, almost forgetting my involvement in today's incident.

"I hope they catch the guy and lock him up for years. It's really scary wondering what will happen next."

"It's probably just—"

"C'mon," Tom interrupts. "Are we gonna play basketball or not?"

I quickly say good-bye to Gwen, and we head through the woods to the courts.

Away from the scene, I exhale loudly. I want to drop to the ground and kiss the dirt. I, Craig Trilosky, am not a killer after all.

Seven

The incident makes the Saturday night news, of course. "Racism in Richmond!" The television reporter is practically frothing at the mouth. Instead of having to cover a boat show or a park opening, he's live at the scene of violence, mystery and racial tension mixed in with a healthy dose of hysteria. The latest incident is being linked to six prior reports of vandalism in the area in the past three weeks. Cars, houses and businesses belonging to Asians had been defaced with racist graffiti. And now the racist's or racists' actions have escalated! Attempted murder! What will the culprits do next? There's some juicy footage of the damaged window in an extreme close-up, an interview with a neighbor who particularly likes the word *shocking* and a sombre statement that no members of the targeted family will speak on camera since they fear for their lives. The news anchor thanks the reporter and holds a grave expression for a split second before introducing the next story about a dispute between a woman who feeds wild birds and her neighbors, who don't appreciate Canada geese frequenting their lawns.

My parents are too caught up in the news to notice the sweat beading my forehead. "That's not far from us, Neil. What's the world coming to?" My mother is about to say more, but my father shushes her. Apparently, the feature on goose droppings has hooked at least one viewer.

I'm quiet all through dinner, not that anyone seems to notice. Margo is whining about how she's the only person she knows who doesn't have a nose or tongue piercing. Mom gasps, but Dad fuels the fire when he wonders aloud if Margo should finish high school at the all-girls Catholic school. Margo throws a predictable hissy fit, Mom tries to soften Dad's threat, and the three go on talking at and over each other. I finish my share of the macaroni casserole and retreat to my room, totally unnoticed.

I slump in my armchair and wonder why I am still friends with a guy who thinks nothing of carrying a gun. Why do I have a friend that wants to see a squirrel die? Isn't that psychotic or some other psychiatric condition? What will he do next? And why don't I have the spine to just say no to his dumb—and dangerous—ideas of what is fun?

Was he always that way? When I first met him, it was all about soccer. Then he got obsessed with basketball. No harm in a couple of guys playing sports, right? Of course, he did make me pull the fire alarm at school in grade two. Okay, he didn't threaten me or anything, but he dared me. He dared me again in grade four. And we had a pretty sophisticated system of swiping candy from people's lunchboxes during "bathroom breaks" when we were in Mrs. Lind's class in grade three. Until Mr. Skye busted us. Maybe I'm the problem. Maybe without a willing accomplice, Tom would be harmless. All talk, nothing else.

Back to today. Tom pulled the trigger, but I'm the buffoon who tackled him. There was something awfully cute about that poor squirrel. I had to do something. Maybe I could have just yelled to make the thing move or to startle Tom and mess up his aim. Yeah, then I could have taken the bullet! I don't know. What good choices are there when your friend takes a gun along for an afternoon of amusement?

Each time I put all the blame on Tom, my conscience twists things up and tells me I'm equally at fault. My conscience seems to speak with my dad's voice.

Later, when I go to bed, I sleep surprisingly well. I feel guilty about it when I wake up at ten the next morning. Tom and I had probably given the new family a restless night. They may have gone to a hotel. How long will it take for them to sleep in peace? When will they stop looking fearfully at cars that pass by their house? I can't get that family out of my mind, even though I don't have any idea what they look like. If I were in their shoes, I'd probably be on edge every second I was at home. Who wouldn't? I wouldn't want to stay inside, but I also wouldn't feel safe out in the community. Hopefully, Gwen's mother and the other neighbors are consoling the family, stepping up their crime watch program and getting to know one another. Maybe something good will come out of this. I try hard to convince myself, but I don't really buy it.

I decide to get out of the house and go for a run. It is raining, and I usually skip running on really soggy days, but I can't stay indoors. I probably deserve to get rained on. Maybe a lightning strike is in the cards too.

Running is therapy for me. No matter how big the problem, it always gets pushed out of my mind five or ten minutes into my run. Running's a lot cheaper and more private than seeing a shrink. Of course, once the run is done, the problem pops back in my head, but for half an hour or so I can block it out.

I run for an hour and ten minutes. I keep going until I start to get a piercing pain in my left knee. That kind of thing always happens when I'm about as far from home as possible. The run back isn't pretty. The rain continues to pour down and soak through my "rain resistant" windbreaker. My right leg takes more of the weight as I run. Eventually, I am hobbling more than running.

Four blocks from home I have to stop. I stumble as my knee almost gives out on a landing. I scream in pain and look around to make sure no one has heard me. Who would have? On a day like today, not even a dog walker is in sight. I limp the rest of the way home—at least, until

I am a couple of houses away. Then I put on a brave face and try to walk normally. If my mom sees me limping, she'll forbid me to run anymore or lecture me on running a reasonable distance or harp at me for wearing too light a jacket or, more likely, combine it all into one long nagfest. Every stride with my left leg is sheer torture. I feel a tear form in the corner of my eye, but I wipe it away and angrily tell myself to suck it up. There's no need to bring out the lightning. That can wait for another day. I'm totally miserable already.

I'm only half surprised that there isn't a squad car in our driveway. What if they've already come looking for me and concluded I was on the run? Maybe a special news bulletin has interrupted regular programming, and my hideous school photo from grade six—the one where my head is tilted and one eye is half closed—has flashed on the screen as an announcer bellows, "Fugitive on the loose! He may look harmless, but he's armed and very, very dangerous! Please, everyone, stay inside and call nine-one-one if you see this criminal."

I decide to go in the back door even though that means I have to pull myself up twelve steps to the back deck. (I've never counted them before, but this time every stair presents a unique daunting challenge.) I hug the railing and try to pull myself up with my upper body to lessen the legwork.

My sister doesn't even look up as I come in. She is slouched on the sofa, hair uncombed, watching a fashion program on TV. Yeah, like that'll help. Well, I guess my criminal status isn't serious enough to interrupt a segment on the latest makeup tips.

Mom is loading the dishwasher and doesn't turn around as she calls out, "Did you have a nice run, dear?" I just grunt and brace myself for climbing the staircase that will lead me to the shower and my room. Right now an elevator seems like the most practical thing in the world to have in a two-story house. Why can't we be more practical?

A few more tears dribble down my face as I stagger up the final three steps. This time I don't bother to wipe them away. I'm too focused on finishing the climb. Can Mount Everest really be worse than this? I can't imagine why anyone would ever bother.

In my room, I peek out my window before getting into the shower. Still no police. My grandfather once said, "Some days you just grimace through." At the time, I thought he was being his usual sour self and referring to things like getting stuck shoe-shopping "just for fun" with my mom and sister. His words now have a far more potent meaning. I can't say I'm glad to understand him a little better.

Eight

Tom hovers impatiently over my desk with his backpack strapped on, waiting for me to gather my stuff. You'd think the bell had rung twenty minutes rather than twenty seconds earlier. It reminds me of those dogs some psychologist trained to drool at the sound of a bell—their reward was a doggy treat. For Tom, basketball is the reward. Miss Chang does not allow us to throw or bounce balls in the classroom, and Tom has to control the urge to begin dribbling until he steps out of the portable. While he hasn't challenged Miss Chang's rule since the first week of school, there seems to be a battle raging between Tom's brain and his hyperactive, basketball-programmed muscles.

"C'mon!" he orders, sounding super-irritated. "Let's get outta here."

I look into his face and make my decision. I'm not moving. I'm still angry with him about the shooting incident and, now that forty-eight hours have passed, I know he's due to do something else that's dangerous and/or foolish. Sorry…not today. At least not with me riding shotgun.

"I'm not going yet. I gotta get extra help on math."

"What? Are you nuts? You want to stay after school to do *more* math?"

"I told you. I don't get it. I need help if I'm going to pass."

"I don't get *you*." Smart comeback. Off he goes in a huff. I pity the younger kids he'll encounter on his way home. But I am relieved. I don't have to get pulled into some crazy stunt. More importantly, I've come clean—not so much about the past, but at least about today and maybe about the future. Tom has no idea that I've been coming early to school every day for the last couple of weeks. Lately, I've been feeling like I finally understand the regular in-class math lessons, but I continue to get extra tutoring just to be sure. Since math has never been my thing, I keep waiting for the heavy fog to settle back in my brain.

Now that he knows, I can stay after school and I won't have to wake up early anymore. Tomorrow, my alarm clock will suffer a little less abuse and the chances have increased by seventy-five percent that I will get to my cereal before it turns to mush. Look at me, using math stats!

I stay away from Tom all week. To be fair, he isn't exactly seeking me out either. At first, we exchange strained hellos, but soon we're ignoring each other completely. Tom seems to go out of his way to show that he can have a good time without me. He does his best to be the class clown, spiking his hair with heavy duty gel, bowling with oranges at lunch, intentionally falling out of his seat a couple of times and performing impromptu finger puppet shows when Miss Chang uses the overhead projector in science. If you ask me, the overhead shadows stopped being funny in grade five, but a lot of the boys and some of the girls still give Tom the audience he craves.

Tom invests a great deal of time trying to impress Erin, Tracey, Taryn, Stephanie and any other girl who screams or otherwise reacts to his teasing and taunting. He thinks he is so cool, but he's never looked more ridiculous.

By Wednesday I've had enough of The Tom Show, so I invite Mark Tam over for lunch. Mark is one of the smart kids. Disgustingly smart at times. Math seems effortless for him. Whenever Miss Chang introduces some new concept, he absorbs it immediately and often raises his hand with a question or comment that extends the concept or applies it to something else. Miss Chang gets all excited about his "terrific question" or "excellent observation." Usually I have to tune him out because I'm still trying to make sense of the basic stuff. Like I said, I'm still on shaky ground with all this math. Tom and I used to make faces every time Mark's hand went up, but I'm beginning to admire him even if I don't have a clue what he's talking about. Maybe I just envy him. Now that I'm actually trying to understand math, I wish I had even half his smarts.

Don't get me wrong though. I'm not having Mark over for lunch so I can con him into doing my homework. A year ago that might've been my motive. Now, I'm determined to figure out the math even if it turns my hair gray by the time I'm fourteen. Mark is actually a nice guy. He even has flaws. He can't really draw, and I remember Mr. Osmond screaming at him a few times last year about incomplete projects.

I first got to know Mark when we had to stay after school once every few weeks because of Desk Dumping. A few minutes before the bell at the end of the day, Osmond would tear through the classroom and dump all the contents of any desk he considered "catastrophically chaotic." Tom only had to stay a couple of times. Surprisingly, his desk was always pretty clean. He told me that he just threw everything out that he didn't feel like organizing. Mark and I were never spared. I didn't learn to be better organized; I just learned to despise Osmond.

Mark never plays basketball, but he's amazing at hockey. I quit hockey two years ago after scoring only two goals for the season. I never figured out how to time my shots so they'd get by the goalie. And I didn't find it satisfying sitting on a bench watching other guys control our team's fate. Still, if Mark is up for some street hockey, it'd be fun to give it another try.

When I told my mom in the morning that Mark would be coming over for lunch, I thought she was going to do a cartwheel or something. Mothers always seem to know who the smart kids are and when they hear you are doing a project or hanging out with one of them, they go berserk, thinking the smart genes will somehow magically rub off on you. As Mark and I walk into the house, the smell of tomato sauce and homemade pizza dough wafts through the front hallway. Yep, Mom is pulling out her best dish to make sure The Genius will want to come back again and again. She starts pouring the soda as soon as she hears the creak of the door. Heck, she's probably been watching from one of the upstairs windows for the first sign of us walking up the street. I can just picture her sprinting down the stairs, skipping every second step, getting in position in the kitchen.

As we eat, she can't help herself.

"How's your mom, Mark? I worked with her on one of the bake sales last year, you know."

"Oh, she's—"

"A very nice woman. No doubt about it. Your sister's going to university next year, isn't she?"

"Yes. That's right," Mark manages to say between mouthfuls.

"She'll be getting a scholarship, won't she? I've heard that she can pretty much go anywhere she wants. Is she going to study premed?"

"Well, I don't—"

"Of course, it's still a little ways away. A lot can change in the next eight or nine months, I suppose. And how are you liking Miss Chang's class? I think she's probably Craig's favorite teacher ever…"

I want to put Mom on mute. How could she blurt that out? Sure, Miss Chang is all right, but how could she tell Mark I really like the teacher? This is one of those times I wish they had trade-ins on mothers. I'd happily take Tom's. His mother never says anything. She'd probably just go off in a separate room and pray that I could keep my smart new friend. That would be awesome. Instead, I have to have a wannabe talk show host as a mom. Of course, she isn't too good at it since she never allows the guest to get a word in. I try to completely tune her out, but I hear her mention that I used to have a sticker collection—WHEN I WAS FIVE, MOM!—and that I belonged to a library club last summer—BECAUSE YOU AND DAD FORCED ME TO!

Mark swallows his pizza even faster than I do. Never has Mom's pizza seemed so utterly tasteless. Embarrassment can drain the flavor out of anything. Mark looks incredibly appreciative when I whisk him off to my dad's office to play a couple of computer games. Fortunately, Mom doesn't follow us. She's too much of a clean freak to let the dishes sit for even a few minutes.

Strangely, Mom's assault doesn't scare Mark off. He's busy after school on Thursday, but he invites me to see a movie with him and Keith Fong on Friday night. Keith has only been in our class for a few weeks. He's from Hong Kong, but his English is pretty good and he seems to have a good sense of humor. My parents don't think twice about letting me go. In fact, Mom gives me twenty-five bucks for the movie and enough popcorn and snacks to share. I buy a large popcorn and pocket the rest of the money for later. If my new social life continues, I'll need it. Sure, my parents will keep funding all my Tom-free events, but it's nice not having to ask.

Nine

he Richmond Racist makes the news again on the weekend. The news anchor peers grimly into our family room, reminding viewers that in the past week anti-Asian graffiti has surfaced on a park bench in the Steveston area and at a Korean mini mall. The reporter who first covered the story is reporting live from another Richmond neighborhood, interviewing a Chinese man who speaks angrily about having the windshield of his new car smashed. There is no reference to graffiti or any sign that the man's car was targeted because he's Asian, but both the man and the reporter blame the Richmond Racist. The camera zooms in on broken glass littering the pavement. Still no leads.

Once again, no one at the house where the "attempted murder" took place will go on camera. My mother shakes her head and mumbles her usual, "What is the world coming to?" as the reporter adds that a special team of officers—the Richmond Anti-Racism Task Force—will aggressively investigate the incidents until the perpetrator, or perpetrators, are brought to justice.

I creep up to my room, worrying about how I will finish grade seven if I have to spend the next twenty years in prison. I envision myself as a heavily tattooed thirty-three-year-old student in a neon-orange jumpsuit, returning to Miss Chang's class. I won't remember any of the math, and every missing pencil will be blamed on me, the ex-con.

As I clutch a pillow and sit on my bed, I tell myself that none of the hysteria is my fault. Tom had taken the gun. He was the one who wanted to skin a squirrel. I'd said no to everything. Well, I had gone with him. And I had fled the scene.

Still, the TV reporter was blowing everything out of proportion. *What'll it be Sunday night, Lois? By gosh, the Richmond Racist has slashed some tires! Tune in at eleven! Richmond Racist writes on picnic table!* Anything racist is despicable. I know that, but since the media has it all wrong about the motive for the shooting, maybe the windshield smashing was random vandalism, not a hate crime. There's got to be a way to make all the craziness go away. A way other than confessing.

My deepest fear is that some horribly violent act will get pinned on the Richmond Racist and that somehow the cops will find out about Tom and me. Maybe in order to close the case and calm the city they will charge us with everything.

I worry that more Asians will be losing sleep or getting angry. Maybe even Miss Chang is upset. What will Mark Tam think if the police haul me in for questioning?

I think about calling the police and coming clean about my part in the shooting. If they believe me, people will learn that the "attempted murder" involved a squirrel, not a person. Maybe the whole media frenzy will wind down. Then again, maybe the media won't want their lead story ruined by a stupid seventh grader. What if they refuse to let the truth be told? Gosh, am I getting even more paranoid? How paranoid do you have to be to be committed? I seem destined for lockup of one kind or another. Still, by confessing, I'll have my dignity—such as it is.

Then I think of Tom beating me to a pulp. Then I think of Tom's dad doing the same to him. If a lima bean sandwich can trigger a whipping, God knows how that man will react if he finds out Tom stole his gun. If I take full responsibility for the window thing, how do I explain where I got the gun? You can't exactly just pick one up at the grocery store or find one in a ditch. Not in my neighborhood anyway…Richmond Racist or not.

I don't have an answer. I feel nauseous, so I clench my pillow against my stomach, hoping that will bring comfort. It's no use. I do the only thing I can think of doing. I turn on my dad's computer and download Space Explorers.

You have a lot of potential as a writer. You have a knack for telling a story and a unique way of describing things.

I read the comments on my story draft once again. There is more, of course. My spelling is a little too creative, my sentences never end, and I need to throw in some apostrophes. (Those are the commas in the air, right? If they called them "flying commas" maybe people would learn how to use them.) But it's the first comment that catches me off guard. Potential? Wow! Everybody else must've turned in really awful stories if Miss Chang is pinning her hopes on me.

My thoughts are interrupted when Miss Chang comes to my desk and, with a huge smile, repeats her positive comments—and outlines the technical problems as well. She gives specific examples to support her claim that I can write. I even used something called *alliteration* although I don't have any idea what that is.

I'm amazed. I still think it must be a fluke. My last writing assignment got a "generous" C-minus. That was the one where I had to add a character to change the plot of the novel. To say that I even skimmed the book would be a stretch. Although Miss Chang had liked the novelty of my adding Big Bird, she'd found "wild inaccuracies" in the basic plot. Apparently they don't sing "The Sun Will Come Out Tomorrow" in a school play in *Anne of Green Gables.* Canadian classic or not, it's a girl book. What did she expect?

Anyway, back to the sudden flash of writing success. Miss Chang is now reading parts of my story sentence by sentence and praising my *writing voice*, whatever that is. No teacher has ever seemed so excited about anything I've done in class. Well, Mrs. Jeter at my old school may have come close in kindergarten when I finished my macaroni sculpture of a seal. Although Miss Chang talks to me privately, she keeps getting louder. It's a little embarrassing, but I don't ask her to stop.

The story I'd handed in was about a couch potato named Gilligan. I took the name from an old TV show. Miss Chang even thinks that is clever, naming a TV addict after a famous television character. I'm not about to burst her bubble by telling her the only reason I came up with it was because I was watching reruns of *Gilligan's Island* while writing.

Anyway, the story begins with Gilligan watching a rerun of *Wheel of Fortune* and solving each puzzle with amazing ease; the show is interrupted by a news bulletin about an escaped murderer. Upset that he's missing a chance to solve the next puzzle, Gilligan goes into a rage and flings a near-empty Cheetos bowl at the TV, accidentally smashing the screen. For the first time in months, Gilligan must find something else to pass the time, so he ventures out into that strange world known as "the outdoors." Naturally, his path crosses with the escaped murderer. Gilligan saves the day, becomes a local hero, buys a new TV and becomes addicted to television news programs. End of story. No big deal.

Miss Chang creates such a fuss that I start to care about turning in a polished final copy. For the first time in—well, ever—I use a class dictionary to not only correct words she'd circled but also to look up words in the extra passages Miss Chang wants me to write.

I'd started out thinking Miss Chang was crazy. Perhaps I'd just lucked out. Is Miss Chang a *Wheel of Fortune* fan? But what if I really do have potential?

I guess Tom got bored doing his own thing. The class clown routine works in the classroom with a captive audience, but I'm sure he wasn't hanging out with anyone after school. Which explains why he's shown up this evening and is trying to sit through my computer game. It's a miserable experience for both of us—he is antsy and bored and I'm impatient because he is so slow at picking up how to play.

"This game sucks," he complains as he damages his shuttle on a rough landing on Neptune. "Why don't they make the spaceship explode?"

"That's not the point—"

"Well, what is the point? We've been playing this game for ten minutes and the biggest thrill has been taking a picture of Epsilon Microscopii in the Microscopium constellation for the Control Center. Whoopee."

"It's about filling your photo log so you can—"

"Yeah, whatever. It's about wasting your time with dots in space that have stupid names stupid people made up. Hey! This one's called Norma! A star called Norma!"

"It's a constellation."

"Whatever. Forget Microscopium. I just renamed it Sue. Norma's best friend. Put that in the photo log."

"That's not what—"

"And I'm renaming your Camelo-something-or-other Bob. Norma's boyfriend. Hi, Bob!"

"Stop it! You're taking all the fun out of it!"

"Fun? This is fun?"

That does it. I quit the game in total frustration. He lets out a mocking "Awww," and tacks on "See ya', Bob!" I sit and sulk for five minutes while he spins in my dad's office chair.

To my surprise, he suggests we go running. Tom hates running, since he doesn't see any purpose in it. No points, no body checking, no ball bouncing. We run a whole kilometer before he makes some excuse about an ankle problem. I don't bother to call him on it. It isn't so bad anyway since we've stopped only a block from McDonald's, and I still have money left from the movies. As we walk, Tom's hobble fades away completely. I guess fries and a shake are a good substitute for physical therapy.

Hanging out with Tom again isn't really so bad. I haven't missed him, but I'm used to him, so we fall back into our old ways without any discussion about how much we'd bugged each other after Squirrel Saturday. It takes a lot less effort to talk with Tom than with Mark. I don't have to think much when Tom and I tell jokes or make fun of people. There's something to be said for familiarity.

Ten

Common sense. Miss Chang mentions it at least five times a day. Where another teacher would automatically yell at Tom as he prepares to spit a mouthful from the water fountain at one of the girls, Miss Chang calmly states, "Use common sense, Tom." Strangely, it almost always works. It sounds better than "Act your age," one of my dad's favorite phrases, even though it basically means the same thing.

As Tom and I are crossing Blair Road after school, a two-door rust bucket with stinky black smoke spewing from the tailpipe comes whirring around the corner and misses me by inches. It would have hit me if I hadn't been training on my sprint starts lately. Tom was walking a couple of paces ahead of me and had already reached the curb.

Naturally, I'm surprised and angry. But Tom is enraged. He grabs a rock and chucks it at the car, hitting the trunk. The driver, who seconds earlier had been in such a hurry, slams on the brakes, does a U-turn and speeds back in our direction.

"C'mon, Tom. Let's get out of here." I know this won't be pretty.

"No way! He tried to kill you."

"Well, he might try again."

"Yeah, but this time we're ready."

Ready? The guy is behind the wheel of a moving vehicle, and Tom has already chucked the only rock to be found. Still, one look at the rage in Tom's eyes and I know better than to say anything.

At this point, I don't think even Miss Chang could've calmed him down. Exhaust fumes have choked any trace of common sense.

The driver storms out of his car, engine still running, smoke still spewing. "You gonna pay for that dent, boy?" he hollers after letting loose a string of profanity.

"Sorry," Tom replies, his voice thick with sarcasm. "I left my piggy bank at home."

"Why, you little—"

What ensues is an exchange of every four-letter word ever created. I utter a few profanities as well, but neither Tom nor the driver seems to know I am there. I sit on the curb and wait.

The big-bellied driver lands the first punch. I can't believe it. The guy must be three times our age and he's taking a swing at a kid. An obnoxious, aggressive kid, but still—a kid. The shot hits Tom on the right cheek, and Tom responds with a punch that sinks deep into the guy's gut. The man grabs Tom's shoulders with both his hands, shakes him and then lifts him off the ground.

"I'm not afraid of you, loser!" Tom says, looking ridiculous yet defiant. Tom takes a well-aimed kick, hitting the man where it counts. The man drops Tom to the ground and topples over in agony.

Erin Patterson's dad comes running over from two houses down and stands between the two. As the driver gets up, Mr. Patterson folds his arms, assumes the position of a roadblock and stares directly into the guy's eyes. "Get out of here before the police arrive. They've been called; don't doubt me."

For all I know, Mr. Patterson may be a former defensive end for the Dallas Cowboys. He is wide, but it isn't on account of rolls of fat. Even a lunatic (or two of them) can tell that this episode is over. The man stares back for a few seconds before hobbling to his car. He tosses out a few more choice phrases, turns his car around and speeds away. I guess if you can burn a little rubber it makes your retreat less humiliating.

Mr. Patterson then turns his gaze on us. "You two are in my daughter's class, aren't you?" he asks sternly, not bothering to see if Tom is all right.

"Yes, sir," I answer.

"You stay away from her. I don't want her mixing with the likes of you. In time, you'll both grow up to

be the spitting image of the sad character that just left."
With that, Mr. Patterson walks back to his yard and
resumes mowing the lawn.

"You all right?" I ask Tom.

"No thanks to you," Tom fumes. He gets up and
walks on. I don't bother catching up. I should have
thanked him, I guess, but I don't really feel thankful.

Trying to be his friend is exhausting. The guy is
totally unpredictable. Maybe Mr. Patterson is right.
Maybe Tom will become that hothead in the car. Maybe
his prediction is true for me too.

Eleven

T he next morning at school, Tom is his usual annoying, loud, chatty self. I go home for lunch because I've forgotten my gym shorts. When I return, he is in a totally foul mood.

As soon as he sees me, he swears and calls me gay.

"Why do you always wanna be near me anyway?" he demands. Funny, because I've been trying to stay away from him. Swinging by the basketball court two minutes before the afternoon bell is obviously my mistake.

"Why don't you like any girls at school?" he persists. I could tell him it's because they spend their lunches looking through celebrity magazines, putting on fingernail polish, planning to go to the mall or talking about last night's phone conversations in play-by-play detail. Why would anyone want to give up running or a computer game for that?

But I don't argue with him. He's back to looking dumb and dangerous: mouth open (tongue thankfully in), eyes bugging out, ball bouncing the whole time.

Something is up. Guys call each other gay to piss each other off, but Tom has never done that to me. It seems to be more than a casual taunt.

I turn and walk away. I've got a couple of French questions I forgot to do for homework anyway.

"That's it," he calls. "Stay away from me, you queer." The nearby conversations shut down now that Tom's big mouth has everyone's attention. I can feel my body shaking. I sense that everyone is looking at me, but I keep my eye on the portable and head inside.

Things are okay in science and French, because I have no contact with Tom. I make sure not to look over at him. Then comes PE.

I wish I'd left my gym shorts at home so I could just sit on the bench. In the change room in front of all the guys, Tom announces, "Better watch it. Craig's looking for a boyfriend." Everyone laughs. I have no idea what to say or do. Should I swear? Punch him? Storm out? Should I knock down everyone who is laughing? Why are they laughing anyway? Are they just relieved that they aren't today's target?

"Shut up!" I reply. Wow. Not very original, but it seems to get everyone's attention. The guys stop laughing. They probably thought I'd laugh it off or take a swing at him. Now maybe they're wondering if Tom is telling the truth.

Tom exits early, throwing out, "Guess I hit a hot spot" as a parting shot. The change room clears quickly. I stay there, dreading the class I usually like best.

By the time I go out, they've finished stretches and are running laps.

"Where've you been, Craig?" Miss Chang asks. Though she tries to look calm, I detect an undercurrent of exasperation. "You missed warm-up."

"I'm not feeling too well," I answer, holding my arms crossed over my stomach.

"Do you need to sit out or go to the nurse's room?"

As she finishes her question, I notice Tom running past me with a big smirk on his face. "No," I say, surprising myself. I had an out and I let it go.

"Well, do the stretches and then rest if you need to," Miss Chang says as she briskly walks away to cheer on the slower runners.

Within a couple of minutes, Miss Chang calls everyone over to divide us into four teams for volleyball. She hasn't even numbered off four people when Tom blurts out, "I'm not playing on Craig's team or against him. Put me in the other game."

"I try to create fair teams," Miss Chang says. "I don't take requests."

As she continues, Tom interrupts again. "I'm not playing anywhere near Craig, and you can't make me. He's in love with me."

Great. First all the guys, now the girls and Miss Chang. If she sends him to the office, he'll find a way to humiliate me over the school's PA system—on the only afternoon my mom is in the building.

Thankfully, Miss Chang directs Tom to sit on a bench while she finishes making the teams. "Do you want to talk about it, Craig?" she asks quietly as I head to my assigned court. I shake my head emphatically. I don't want anyone to see a teacher bailing me out.

We rally for serve and play a couple of points when a girl on my team hits an errant bump which flies sideways and out of bounds. Tom leaps up from the bench, retrieves it and intentionally drills it at my head. I duck in time. Miss Chang doesn't see it, since she is on the other court patiently helping Mindy Chu figure out how to get a serve over the net.

I do my best to ignore Tom and focus on game play. In the middle of the next point, Tom pounces on me and knocks me down. The punches are flying so fast all I can do is get my hands up to block my face.

In less than a minute, Miss Chang and a couple of the guys pull Tom off me.

At least a dozen eyes peer down at me. Could someone please pull the fire alarm and get them away from me? I am lying on the floor, too stunned to do anything other than lift my head ever so slightly. One of the girls screams about blood on the gym floor—apparently from the back of my head. I rest my head again and surrender to being the main attraction of the day's freak show. At least I have the sense to close my eyes. The principal rushes in, and I tilt my head to see her escorting Tom away.

Miss Chang applies a cold wet paper towel to my face as my mother fusses over me. Wonderful. Rescued by my teacher and my mom. When I start to sit up, I throw up.

After fifteen minutes in the nurse's room, my mother takes me to the doctor to have things checked out. I've got some bruises and I have a small gash somewhere at the back of my head. A big bump too. If you're gonna have a wound, it's always best for it to be in a place where you don't have to look at it.

As we drive home from the doctor's office, my mom's too upset to talk. She focuses really hard on traffic. I try to figure out what brought on Tom's latest outburst. What was he thinking? Was something going on at home? And, if so, is that any excuse? We've been friends for ages, and he suddenly goes delusional and gets it in his head I'm gay? I can't explain it. That's the thing. I'm not sure even Tom can.

At home, my mother informs me that Tom has been suspended for two days. That means he'll have a four-day weekend. Harsh. I just want to know how I can transfer.

Twelve

At 7:15 the next morning, the phone rings. I'm eating my standard fare of soggy Shreddies when my mom answers it.

"Hello? Yes. What do you want?" Wow! Mom sounds terse. Obviously, the coffee hasn't kicked in. If she asks me to take out the garbage, I'll do it without the routine complaining. "I'm sure he doesn't want to talk to you," she says. Something bad must've happened with Dad at work yesterday. Even so, he wouldn't want Mom talking to his clients like that. This isn't the day for him to be trying for the perfect shave. "No, I'm sure—No—" Bang! Wow. I've never seen Mom hang up on anyone. Dad does it every so often when business talks get too intense, and now Mom's acting like Dad's agent.

"Who was it, Mom?"

"Tom."

As she answers me, I see the bags under her puffy eyes. Worse, her eyes are all red. She looks like she hasn't slept, and I bet she's had a good cry before breakfast.

"I don't want you hanging out with him anymore." Her voice is strong and her words firm. This is not the time to protest. I don't want to anyway.

The phone rings again. I bow my head to watch the slimy cereal bits fracture in my bowl. I've lost my appetite, so I just maneuver my spoon here and there between the wheat particles. For a moment, I regress and the spoon becomes a shiny racing boat. The phone continues to ring. Mom pours another cup of coffee, ignoring my lapse in maturity and the persistent ringing of the phone. After nine or ten rings, Dad yells from upstairs for someone to get the phone.

Mom finally picks up. I know immediately that Tom has had the nerve to call back. Mom's voice and stance remind me of a mama grizzly, determined to protect her cub. Or maybe a female wrestler, ready to toss her foe overhead and out of the ring. (Okay, so I flip channels on Saturdays! It's not like I've ever watched a whole bout.)

"I have told you quite clearly that he does not want to speak to you." Every syllable is delivered like a strong punch.

"I'll take it, Mom," I say. I don't want to talk to him, but I want to hear what he has to say. How pathetic and desperate will his apology be? In disgust, Mom drops the phone on the counter, walks to the sink and lets the garbage disposal be her substitute screamer.

"Craig, you gotta come by my house on the way to school."

"You're suspended."

"But my dad doesn't know. I have to act like I'm going to school."

"You're out of luck."

"C'mon, man! He'll kill me. I mean, really kill me."

"I can't help you. Bye."

Incredible. Twenty-four hours earlier this guy was my best friend, like it or not. Now I'm feeding him to the wolves—or one drunken werewolf anyway. I didn't know I could be so cold. I guess that's what a blow to the head'll do. I stir the mess in my bowl a couple more times before deciding breakfast is over. As I get up and leave the kitchen, I feel Mom's stare following me. I know she wants to unload some motherly advice, but she wisely resists. It would be too awkward trying to discuss what Tom did yesterday and, worse, why he'd done it. I'm sure that the principal filled her in on all the details, but I prefer to pretend she knows nothing.

I take a different route to school just to avoid going anywhere near Tom's house. Why does he need me to pretend to walk to school with him? It's not as if we walk to school together every day. Most times, yes, but not always. Besides, just yesterday he was all psychotic about being seen with me. What's changed? Maybe it's a trick to get me over there so he can finish what he started.

Tom hadn't said anything close to "I'm sorry" on the phone. He was just trying to save his neck. I have my own neck to worry about. I have to walk back into class after my best friend went berserk and declared that I'm gay. I decide to walk really slowly so I won't get to class until the moment the bell rings. No point in subjecting myself to any more torment than absolutely necessary.

How bad can it be if Tom's dad finds out what happened yesterday? Would he beat Tom? As far as I know, his older sister and brothers were worse than Tom in school and they're still alive—well, at least two of them are. I still don't know a thing about where the oldest brother is. Tom refuses to talk about what happened to Andy.

My thoughts are interrupted by the school bell. I'm still a block away. How did I mistime it so badly? Being late will attract even more attention than arriving early. This is great—just great.

When I walk in, Miss Chang is already going over the integer homework in math. That woman doesn't waste a single second of school time. Work, work, work. Come to think of it, that's a good thing today.

"Good morning, Craig," Miss Chang chirps, just as I'd hoped she wouldn't. Why is it that teachers have no clue what it's like to be a student?

Miss Chang immediately resumes demonstrating math problems, leaving me to face the stares and glares of my peers. Strangely though, most people don't turn my way at all. Mark gives me a half wave before focusing again on the lesson. Todd Allbright smiles briefly from across the room as do one or two others. Mindy Chu stares for a few moments, but I glare at her like always and she goes back to looking at the blackboard.

"You okay?" Jenny Tai whispers from the desk behind me.

"Yeah."

"Good. I'll show you the homework question you missed."

That's nice of her. To my surprise, everyone is perfectly normal all morning. Then, it hits me. Of course! Miss Chang. With my early departure yesterday and Tom being booted from school, she'd pounced on the opportunity to give the class one of her famous pep talks. I can almost hear her: "How would it feel if it had been you?" "What do you think Craig's feeling right now?" "This is a remarkably mature class that knows how to show respect to each of its members. I expect nothing less."

Maybe in her trademark fashion, Miss Chang had nipped things in the bud and saved me. She's that rare breed: a do-gooder who actually does good. Even if I'd wanted to thank her, she wouldn't have let me—not when we have algebraic equations with negative integers to learn.

Thirteen

I'm always tired on Mondays. Just when I get into the swing of sleeping in on Saturday and Sunday, along comes Monday to spoil it all. Why can't school start at eleven in the morning? Of course, I wouldn't want it to run longer either. Maybe they could stop teaching math, science and French. Later start, shorter day. Works for me.

This particular Monday morning is worse than most. My mother barges into my room, screaming at me to turn the alarm off. I never knew it was on. With vocal cords like hers, who needs the alarm anyway?

Over breakfast, my mother is reciting all the things I need to do at home after school. I fall asleep on the table shortly after she mentions shovelling some manure. Boy, does that make her mad. I get my second awakening of the day from those lungs. No amount of fatigue is worth hearing Megaphone Mom again.

At school, I realize I've left my backpack at home. Here I'd spent hours (well, maybe twenty minutes) on my homework, and I'm not going to get credit for it. The math work wouldn't have mattered since I haven't understood a thing about negative integers in equations over the past week. I'm just waiting for the unit to end. Why would anybody want to subtract (12) from $(-9x)$ in the first place? Who thought that up? Four-year-olds are freaked by monsters; for seventh graders, it's mathematicians.

I'm so tired that it's not until the math homework is assigned that I realize Tom isn't there and remember why.

I have no regrets about this latest Tom Break. When a guy yells at you and beats you up in front of the whole class, it's pretty easy to enjoy the downtime. A suspension might make Tom think about his actions. Maybe it'll give him time to come up with a sincere way to apologize and explain himself. That's why, when I see Tom rolling his basketball like a bowling ball along the curb and trying to knock over empty trash cans, I don't look for an alternate route home. He stops his odd little game as I approach. He looks right at me. He's probably giving his apology one last run-through in his head. I stop right in front of him and wait to hear what he has to say.

He punches me.

Ah, yes. The suspension has clearly had the desired effect.

"Lay off," I say. "We're not friends anymore. And just to set the record straight, I'm not gay! Where'd that come from? Don't know what kind of short circuit happened in your brain, but you really lost it." I should keep walking, but I don't.

Tom stands there, smirking. "Shut up."

"Get out of my sight. I mean it." I make a move to the left to pass him, but he shifts to block.

"No, you don't."

"I do too. Why'd you have to say those things?" Okay, mouth, stop extending the conversation. I shift right; he blocks again. For a guy who accused me of being gay, he seems desperate to be my dance partner.

"I didn't mean it."

"Well, why'd you have to not mean it in front of absolutely everyone?"

"Get over it, all right?" He continues to lateral left and right, thankfully dribbling the basketball so it doesn't feel so stupid. "We're friends."

"Yeah, right. Why'd you hit me just now?"

"Because you deserved it."

"You're totally whacked. I oughta be hitting you."

I head to the other side of the street and walk on. Tom doesn't follow.

Walking home, I am more mad at myself than at Tom. What is wrong with me? Did I really think Tom would apologize? The only times I've ever heard him say sorry are when a teacher or Mr. Skye makes him.

He doesn't ever mean it. He just does it so he can get back to playing basketball at lunch. Even the teachers must know that. They don't want to spend all their lunches babysitting the guy.

He doesn't even pretend to apologize to me. He punches me. Sure, it wasn't hard or anything, but after what happened in the gym, how can he think that's the way to fix things?

Why do I keep giving Tom a chance? Yeah, he's funny. Yeah, he makes life interesting. But come on! All my office visits were one thing, but now it's guns and fights with adults and gay taunts and fights with me. We've got history. Lots of it. But friendships change, right? Things would be so much easier if there was some other place where I really fit in.

Fourteen

om's return to school comes without balloons or welcome banners.

"I'M BAAAACK!" he bellows, causing our classmates to glance his way, grimace and then resume whatever they'd been doing. Fours days of reflection have not helped Tom discover how to win friends.

Surprisingly, nobody looks to see my reaction when Tom walks in. I guess there's no reason to do so. There isn't a person in the room who hasn't at one time or another been subjected to Tom's intimidation tactics. Last week I was the victim and that gave everyone else a break. If he had put me into a coma and been suspended for a whole week, the class would have been a little more grateful. I have no doubt that, if the school held a fundraiser to ship Tom off to Guatemala instead of carrying on with its Adopt-A-Child program, we'd be cheering "Bon Voyage" (or whatever you'd say in Spanish) in a matter of days.

I have no contact with Tom the whole day. Miss Chang has created a new seating arrangement: Tom's desk is right beside hers and mine is way over on the opposite side of the room. It's a nice gesture, but a little subtlety would have been appreciated. She could've put me in the second row from the right instead of the farthest. Having a tiny female teacher protect me is just plain embarrassing.

As long as I am away from Tom, it doesn't really matter where I sit. I really don't have any other friends in the class. I haven't done anything with Mark since we went to the movies. He's always in the computer lab during lunch and recess. I like computers, but not at school. The lab has too many bad memories—lots of typing drills and lame assignments by teachers who don't know much about technology. The times I do go in the lab, Mark and Lewis Tsai are too consumed by whatever website they're on to notice. Keith is starting to hang out pretty much exclusively with a group of Chinese ESL students, and there's no use trying to mix with them because they always speak Chinese. If I stand near them, nothing changes. I guess if my family moved to Hong Kong and I found a group of students who spoke English, I'd act the same way.

For the past couple of days, I've been eating at my desk by myself with a book open. I'm not really reading. I'm kind of spying on everyone else, listening in on their conversations and watching what they do. It's time I figured out how normal people my age interact. Each group seems totally oblivious to everyone and everything else in the room, making my eavesdropping not much of a challenge.

I'm not the only one eating alone. Mindy is always by herself. If you ask me, she's someone who doesn't know how to have fun. She always has her head buried in a textbook, diligently trying to do a bonus assignment or reading ahead in Social Studies.

Roger Battersby also eats solo. There's nothing really wrong with him, but then again there's nothing really right. He's just flat-out boring. He never has any ideas of his own. I hate having him in my group for any projects because he never contributes anything. He just listens and shrugs his shoulders a lot. His face goes beet red whenever he has to speak in class, and he makes talking look utterly painful. He's been a favorite target of Tom's because it's so easy to see when you've gotten under his skin.

The big surprise is that Taryn is eating alone. That one I can't figure out at all. She is one of the popular girls—along with Tracey, Erin and Tammi. But now she looks completely miserable. She isn't used to it the way Mindy and Roger are. Tracey, Erin and Tammi sit close to her and act as if she doesn't exist. They laugh louder than ever and make every effort to look as if they are having the best time ever. Taryn silently finishes her lunch and then aimlessly walks the halls until the afternoon bell rings. The other three always calm down once Taryn makes her exit.

It might be the perfect opportunity to befriend Taryn, but I know there is no point in trying. Even as a loner, she is still way too popular for someone like me.

With Tom back in school, I could go back to eating with him, but I'd rather eat by myself. Tom has big problems. He needs help. Even I have figured that out. Shock treatments might not do any good, but I'm at the point where I wouldn't mind watching. Maybe he'll eventually get sent off to military school and get ordered around by tough, battle-scarred men. Why do they put problem guys in the military anyway? Does it really make sense to teach them how to use weapons?

In truth I don't have to try to ignore Tom, because he is apparently doing the same to me. At the sound of the recess and lunch bells, he vanishes faster than teachers do when there's a problem on the playground. I have no idea what he is doing, and I'm glad to have it that way.

Fifteen

om's return to school doesn't last long. Mrs. Brewer pulls him out of class, and then he is gone. I figure he'd mouthed off to Vice-Principal Skye one too many times and the school decided to take a stand.

Nobody in class voices any concern or curiosity. Life goes on. I don't bother to call him to get his side of things, because I am pretty tired of hearing his side: The whole world is against him, and there is no way he is responsible for anything. Still, after he's been gone for five days, I start to think of phoning. I wonder if they've forced him to transfer to another school in the district or if they've kicked him out completely.

I'm in my room finishing up an essay on the value of tombs and pyramids in ancient Egypt when my mother calls out, "Craig! Your friend's on the news!" At first I think she's referring to Mark—maybe he's receiving some award for Smartest Student Ever—but as I run down the stairs, she yells, "Come quickly!"

I've missed the whole story by the time I get to the den. My mother's face looks pale as she stands there, looking back and forth from the TV to me. The phone rings before I can get anything out of her.

"Get that, will you?" she asks absentmindedly.

I grab the phone in the den and can't get a "Hello" out before the voice from the other end says, "Craig? Is Craig there, please?"

I recognize the voice despite the total absence of a giggle. It's Tracey. I play it cool. "This is Craig. Who's this?"

"Hi, Craig. It's Tracey from school. Did you see the news? Tom's missing." I don't say a thing. I know she isn't kidding. The expression on my mother's face provides confirmation.

Tracey goes on and on, talking faster than I can follow at times. This is grade seven drama of the highest kind, and I know that she will have a lot more calls to make tonight.

"Can you believe Tom had a gun? Tom! Miss Chang moved him into the row near me. Do you think he ever had the gun at school? You know, in his desk or his backpack? Everyone says he liked me, you know. Isn't that creepy? The guy had a gun! And where is he now? He could be in the bushes out back right now! Freaky! I don't think I'm going to be able to sleep tonight! Maybe he's run off to the States. Or he could've snuck on a ferry to Victoria. God, the farther the better!"

Presumably, she's called me first because I might have the inside scoop, but as she rambles on with all sorts of wild possibilities, I realize I could leave the phone on the counter and she'd never know the difference. She closes with an abrupt, "Oh, wait till Erin hears! Gotta go!" I let the phone hum a little in my ear before sitting down with Mom. She fills in the missing pieces.

Tom has run away. The reporter called him the "accidental" Richmond Racist—a wannabe squirrel killer but not a racist maniac. Tom confessed to the shooting, and the police had no reason to believe he was connected to any of the other incidents. Since the gun was his father's, Tom's homelife had to be investigated; the investigation revealed evidence of abuse, and Tom was headed for foster care. But Tom escaped through his bedroom window while he was supposed to be grabbing a few items to take to the foster home. All this happened four days ago. The press had finally been alerted because the police were now genuinely concerned about Tom. The reporter obligingly stated that the boy did not have his father's gun since it had already been seized, and that he was not considered a threat to the public. The reporter had obviously never set foot in Miss Chang's classroom.

My mom starts crying. "To think he was one of your friends!" she says. "He could've shot you by accident with that gun. Oh, what if he'd had that thing in the gym that day? Why in the world did they have a gun lying around the house? That boy's father should be in jail. You haven't heard from Tom, have you?"

"No."

"You don't know where he is?"

"No."

"Well, I hope nothing bad has happened to him. Heaven knows what that boy will get into, living on the streets. A foster home would've been the best thing for him."

At night, I sleep a little, but I'm awake to see every hour go by on the clock. I am totally confused about what I've been told, what I haven't been told and what I know. What had made Tom confess about the gun incident? It had to have happened when Mrs. Brewer pulled him out of class. Why hadn't I been called down to the office too? Had Tom taken full blame and protected me? Why was he slated for foster care? Had his dad beaten him again? Where had he run off to? Why hadn't he told me any of this? Why didn't he ask me for help?

I feel sick to my stomach, worrying about Tom and feeling guilty about how I hadn't even bothered to call to check up on him. Even though I am sure Tom can face any situation on his own, that doesn't mean he deserves to. I was equally responsible for the whole squirrel fiasco, and now his life is in chaos while I continue my safe existence.

I decide to set the record straight first thing in the morning.

Sixteen

I stop by the office as soon as I arrive at school. The secretary blocks my path to Mrs. Brewer's office. Perhaps she is under strict orders to keep all seventh-grade hoodlums away. To most adults, all seventh graders are potential hoodlums.

"Mrs. Brewer is in a meeting right now, Craig."

Whoa. She knows my name. I guess I've earned my share of Frequent Office Points. "This is urgent. I have to talk to her."

"Why don't you talk to Mr. Skye? I think he just headed down the hall."

Yeah, right. He'd double my suspension and send me off to a foster family too. He'd call an assembly, have me sit in the front facing the audience and lead everyone in a repeated chant of "Shame!" I stand my ground and insist on seeing Mrs. Brewer.

"Try checking back at recess." What she really means is, Go on. Get out of my office. She grabs a file and turns her back to me as she opens it and straightens the papers inside.

"Could you please have me called out of class as soon as she's available?"

The gatekeeper is losing her patience. "What is this about? We can't have you missing classes because of a lost basketball or a bad grade—"

"It's about Tom Hanrahan."

Her eyes widen. She hesitates; then she nods soberly and says, "I'll give her the message as soon as she's free." The phone rings and she answers it while continuing to watch me in case I make an attempt to burst into Mrs. Brewer's office. I really want to get it over with. What could be more important? I'm ready to confess, and I don't want to have to sit in class pretending everything is fine.

It had occurred to me at exactly 3:17 in the morning that if I took my fair share of the blame for the squirrel scare maybe Tom wouldn't be in such hot water. Maybe his dad would cool down. Maybe the foster family thing would be abandoned. Maybe Tom would come back. At 3:17 in the morning, that sounded like a perfectly reasonable series of maybes. In the light of day, it all seems too ridiculous, too much like the last five minutes of a television movie of the week. Perhaps Tom had snuck across the border—there was no wall or fence, after all—and hitchhiked to Seattle. He could pass for sixteen and get a job at McDonald's. Was I needlessly setting myself up for trouble?

The one thing that seems clear is that Tom has unfairly taken the heat for our part in the Richmond Racist ordeal. I have to do what I can to help him.

Even though the five-minute-warning bell has already gone, most of my classmates are still crowded around the outside steps as I approach the portable. I stop and wait, wanting them to go in before I get any closer. I know why they are there. This is the best gossip of the year, and no one wants to miss out on giving his or her own take on "the real Tom Hanrahan."

Then I spot Vice-Principal Skye talking to a woman with a notebook and a man with an elaborate camera. Tracey is trying her best to talk over Skye and the woman, who are in a heated discussion. With a broad sweep of his right arm, Skye causes half the crowd to back up a few inches. His face is redder than a sunburnt lobster as he forces the woman backward down the stairs and away from the students.

"Get in the classroom…now!" He orders my class-mates without looking back to address them. The photog-rapher snaps wildly as he retreats with his colleague.

"My name has an *e* in it. I hate when it's misspelled. T-R-A-C-E-Y," shouts the gossip queen as she disappears into the portable.

I take a wide loop on the field to avoid Skye and his foes, but I am close enough to hear him fiercely spouting something about "school policy" and "respecting the personal space of minors." Every syllable resonates with authority.

In the classroom, it's total madness. Only three or four people are in their seats. Many are gathered around

Miss Chang, talking all at once. Others huddle in small packs around the room. I check the clock to see if it's me or everyone else who is out of whack. Class should've started two minutes ago. I can picture Tom smiling with satisfaction at the thought that he has taken a chunk out of a regular day's education.

Finally, Miss Chang tells everyone to take their seats. It takes three commands over the course of a couple of minutes before things settle down. Only then do I notice the woman standing quietly at the front of the room. She looks vaguely familiar, and I assume she is a parent or a substitute something. Miss Chang writes *Mrs. Nakashima* on the board as she introduces the woman as a school counselor. Mrs. Nakashima smiles faintly and attempts to make eye contact with the people on the right side of the room. Still, her gaze seems to fly a few centimeters over everyone's head. I can't imagine how such an obviously timid person could possibly assist anyone with a serious problem, but I guess she is the best the school can come up with.

Miss Chang explains that, due to Tom being missing, we will talk as much as we need to about any worries or concerns we have. Mrs. Nakashima nods her head a few times but adds nothing. We are invited to share our thoughts.

"Do you think he's dead?" Marvin Ho blurts out with more excitement than concern. Apparently, with Tom gone, the position of class jackass is up for grabs.

"How can you even say that?" a horrified Mindy Chu chimes in, taking the bait.

"What?" Marvin continues, defensively. "I've never known anyone my age to die. It would just be kinda weird."

Miss Chang tries to move things along as the counselor stares silently at the bulletin boards in the room. No matter what Miss Chang says or does, Marvin has set the mood. Half the class says things like, "His dad coulda hunted him down, shot him and buried him," and, "Maybe he used the gun other times." The others make the whole thing about them. Tracey repeats how freaked she is to have sat near a guy with a gun, and Tammi carries on with, "I just can't believe it! I've never known anyone who had a gun! This is the first time I've known someone who made the news in, like, a bad way." Tom would have put them all in their places with one glare, one stinging comment, one loud guffaw. I keep my mouth shut and glance toward the door, waiting for Mrs. Brewer to come and take me away from this sad circus. Confessing is starting to seem a little less scary.

"I bet Craig knows where he's hiding." Erin's accusation jolts me to alertness. Everyone is looking at me. I say nothing. No one else does either, but they continue to stare.

Couldn't we please do some math? Or look words up in the dictionary or start a massive research project?

Why is nothing happening? Why is everyone still looking at me? Why can't I just tune them all out and be like Mrs. Nakashima, staring into space over everyone's heads?

"If anyone knows anything about Tom, they should speak privately to their parents, myself, Miss Chang, Mr. Skye or Mrs. Brewer as soon as possible." She speaks! Suddenly all eyes swivel toward Mrs. Nakashima. I finally find a spot on the board—the comma between the day and the year for today's date—and tune everything else out. Mrs. Brewer…why hasn't she called me down yet?

Jenny Tai's bizarre suggestion about selling chocolate bars to start a reward fund brings me back from my comma coma. A couple of people start debating whether M & M's or Twix bars will sell more.

A voice at the back of my row breaks in, "I don't want him to come back." Everyone, including me, turns and looks at Roger Battersby. It's the first time he's volunteered anything all year. He stares blankly ahead, breathing heavily and adding nothing more. There is no reason to be all that surprised by his simple statement. Tom had taken pleasure in taunting Roger for the last two years. Roger was such an easy target. Suddenly, he gets up and walks out of the room. Mrs. Nakashima follows.

Keith adds to Roger's comment, saying in perfect English, "I don't want him to come back either. My mom says he hates Chinese people." Another remarkable comment. It is the first time Keith has spoken in class except during math lessons.

Stephanie tries to temper things. "I'm not saying he's not a jerk. I didn't like him either, but he's gotta have some nice qualities. He's just had a hard life. My mom said his older brother killed someone and is in prison. She also said she knows one of their neighbors, and they hear screaming coming from the house all the time. Cops are there once or twice a month, but they never do anything."

"I heard his brother killed *three* people. And my mom says everyone knows his dad's a drunk," Tracey pipes up. I wonder if she shared her insights with the reporter earlier. Clearly, she is relishing every opportunity to inform the public.

Miss Chang tries to tame the talk, but the discussion speeds recklessly along.

"Just because you have a hard life doesn't mean you have to take it out on others," Mark chimes in. "And why would you take it out on animals? Why would he kill squirrels?"

"He didn't!" Uh-oh. Did I say that out loud? Yep. Everyone is looking at me again. I can't wait any longer to talk to Mrs. Brewer. "I stopped him." As people start whispering I stand up and say, "Miss Chang, may I go see Mrs. Brewer?" I'm pushing the door open before she gives her consent.

Seventeen

That night, I realize there is a dead bug squished on the ceiling of my room. It's a bit of a mystery. I can't recall killing it. My sister and my mother both scream at the sight of a bug. My dad…well, he hasn't stepped foot in my room since the day we moved in. The bug left a fairly big smudge mark. I'm guessing it was a spider, but it could have been something more exotic, like a blue-winged African horsefly that arrived inside a crate from Mozambique. Poor bug. It probably never even wanted to come to North America. And look at the welcome it received. Squished by a shoe or a newspaper, unrecognizable even to its family.

Up until now, I haven't spent much time staring at my ceiling. Now I've got plenty of time for that. I'm grounded. Big time! With my dad out of town, Mom imposed the punishment. Dad is typically the severe one, but when she set the term at two months I realized that somewhere way back in her family tree there must have been a hanging judge. It's not just the length of the sentence: The conditions are harsher than anything in prison. No phone calls. It's not like I call a lot of people, but being told I *can't* call makes me want to start up a conversation with Mark or Keith…or even Mindy Chu. It won't happen. My phone has been yanked from the wall and taken who knows where. No TV. Ouch. No music…well, not on my stereo at least. I watched in shock as she pulled each plug and carried the whole system away in two trips. She reached for my pathetic little clock radio and then reconsidered. If it hadn't had an alarm, I'm sure she would have taken it too. She won't even let me eat dinner downstairs! The first meal in my room was undercooked macaroni and cheese and a hot dog with mustard and ketchup, but I'm sure she gave some thought to bread and water. I'm locked up; just me and a dead bug.

Do you think he's dead? What I had dismissed as a callous remark starts to haunt me in the middle of my second consecutive sleepless night. The past few nights have been cold enough for the furnace to be working over-time. Can a person freeze to death? I've seen homeless people in cold weather, but they usually have blankets or big furry dogs. I can't picture Tom packing a blanket before making his great escape. Is his dog, Archie, still at home? How can a person keep warm on a night like this without shelter?

The sleep deprivation brings a more gruesome scene to mind. Mr. Hanrahan, so angry at having his prized gun seized, finds Tom hiding in Archie's doghouse, drags him out and beats him to death. I curl up really tight, trying to make the awful thought go away, but I can almost hear Tom crying out over Archie's puzzled yelps. I'm shocked by how easy it is to imagine the whole thing. If Tom's brother killed someone, isn't it possible that his dad would do the same? Who would ever know? To the rest of the world, Tom has simply run away.

I force myself to think about happy things, good memories of Tom. Last summer he told some jerks at The Zone that we were in grade nine, and then they challenged us to a game of bowling, winners to take twenty bucks. I spent the whole game throwing nothing better than a few spares, too worried about how we were going to pay up if we lost and wondering if the bet was for twenty bucks *total* or *each*. Tom's three strikes and a spare were enough to pull out a win, and we spent the prize playing video games for the next three hours. I asked Tom how he got so good at bowling, and he said it was the only place his dad could take the family on weekends and down a couple of pitchers of beer at the same time.

Which brings me right back to Mr. Hanrahan: heavy drinker, possible killer?

I remember how we biked to Steveston with Archie running beside us. That crazy lab started chasing sea gulls at Garry Point and plunged in the water after one. With the bird long out of sight, Archie continued swimming, despite our frantic calls. Tom tossed off his shoes and shirt and went in after the dog. Knowing I was a better swimmer, I followed in the chilly water. Eventually, Archie started swimming in circles and, once he saw me, started making his way back. We sat on the shore, trying to dry off in a suddenly cool wind and then walked our bikes back, too tired to pedal. Archie kept running ahead and leaping at anything and everything that moved.

Thinking of Archie reminds me of my imaginary murder scene. I can't make the horrible possibility go away. In my mind, Mr. Hanrahan is a serial killer who is responsible for the death of every milk carton kid in the last thirty years. Exhausted and scared witless, I flick the lights on and doodle aimlessly on a pad of Post-its, being careful to make sure none of the scribbles can possibly resemble anything whatsoever. A couple of hours later, my alarm blares, and I am relieved to have to get up, go to school and forget about trying to sleep.

At school, I suddenly know what it's like to be popular. Everyone wants to talk to me, but I don't for a minute kid myself that they have taken a genuine interest in me. They don't care about my running or my thoughts on music any more than they ever have. They always start out with some lame personal questions, but it is all just a lead-up to the inevitable inquisition.

Do you know where he is? Did you ever see his dad beat him? What does squirrel meat taste like?

At recess, I am wanted in every clique in seventh grade. I would take Tom over any of them. He'd be dissing my double dribbling. Or maybe he'd be making fun of the cartoon decals on some poor kid's backpack. Maybe we'd be laughing over a fart joke—so much so that he'd spit half his mouthful of Oreos all over his T-shirt. For all his faults, at least Tom isn't fake. Whether he's punching me out or begging me to watch a Raptors game on TV, I always know where I stand.

I slip back in with Mark and Keith, who hang out with kids from the other grade seven class: Cindy Tan, Lewis Tsai and a new kid named Doris Lee. Being in solitary confinement at home, I stick it out with this group even though it takes a lot of effort to feel included. Keith spouts off in Cantonese the second he's out of class, as if suddenly relieved of the pressure to think in a new language. Doris's English is even worse than Keith's, so the others never even attempt to say anything in English to her. Mark and Cindy, when they aren't consumed by their own private conversations, automatically speak in Cantonese for the benefit of Keith and Doris. Ten minutes can go by without any apparent acknowledgment that I am there. I have no idea why Keith and Mark wait for me at the beginning of each lunch and recess. Maybe it's because I'm pretty approachable when Tom's out of the picture. Maybe it's my sense of humor. Maybe they feel sorry for me.

Miraculously, my mom caves ever-so-slightly on her harsh sentencing. Pleas for TV and the stereo are still premature, but I regain the right to go running after giving several impassioned speeches on the importance of fresh air, fitness and success in sports. Dad wouldn't have budged. Thankfully, a "critical" meeting in Prince George has extended his absence a few more days.

Eighteen

I go running without my sister one Saturday. It's not like I have to run with Margo. It has just become a habit. It isn't any sort of bonding experience. She's seventeen and I'm twelve. She still thinks I'm an immature pest and I think she's—well, just plain strange. Margo's a prisoner of the cosmetics industry. When not getting facials at department store counters, she's inviting friends over to try on one of the thirty or forty shades of red lipstick she has. Back in kindergarten, red was red. She'd save a lot of money if she remembered that.

When we run, we just grunt or move along in silence. I guess there's a purpose though. Knowing that someone else expects you to run kind of makes it difficult to skip. The hardest part about running is getting started.

Anyway, my sister isn't exactly devastated when I say I want to run on my own in the morning instead of waiting until the afternoon. She continues to stare at a music video while smearing her fingernails with fresh nail polish—Tokyo Sunset, I think.

Mom has gone to pick up Dad at the airport and, since they usually go out for a coffee afterward, that gives me extra time out of the house. Seventeen-year-olds have no concept of time, especially when they're parked in front of a television set, so I'm not worried about my sister ratting me out. I run my normal course for a few blocks and then go off in the direction of the Richmond dikes. I'm off to find Tom.

If he's still in Richmond, I figure he's in one of four places. The most obvious is an old shack off Blundell Road just past Railway. We'd hung out there in the summer when he was in his smoking phase, swiping a few cigarettes each day from his sister.

I'm not surprised the building is still there, despite not having seen it in months. Even though it looks like one good gust could blow it away, the shack is a survivor. Stepping through the doorless entrance, I see no trace of Tom or anything that shows the place has been recently occupied. Spray-painted messages cover the walls, but there don't seem to be any new contributions. Most of it makes no sense. Tom says they are gang tags, but I've never seen any gang types hanging around. My favorite graffiti is in dark green paint in the top corner to the right of the doorway: *Anne Murray Rules!* Tom had never heard of her, but my parents forced me to listen to her when we drove to see my aunt and uncle in Vernon. Either a gang member had a really odd sense of humor or my dad was taking a crack at life in the underworld.

Not cool. At any rate, the place is littered with broken beer bottles with faded labels, but that is it.

I move on to an old cottage only a few feet from the dike. It is lived in by an elderly couple who both have poor vision and hearing. There is a crawlspace under the back of the house that Tom and I used to climb into. We only went there a couple of times last summer, but it had been a spot to take refuge on the rare day when it was too hot. We were never caught, although a fat cat once gave us a scare. The place is darker and mustier than I remember. With no sign of Tom, I quickly crawl back out.

The other possible places are over by McDonald Beach and the Iona Island sewage plant. There is no way I can run there. Tom and I always biked, and I'll have to wait for another day when I can escape from the Trilosky penitentiary.

I don't know what I was thinking when I went off on a solo search party. He's been gone more than two weeks. He's bound to be far from Richmond by now. Even though he only got one shot on the news and a front-page picture in the community paper, someone would have spotted him if he'd stayed too close to home. Still, it's incredibly frustrating not knowing for certain if he's okay. As much as I try to convince myself he's fine, there are enough what-ifs to drive me crazy.

No one at school mentions him now that the media hype has died down. I don't get how everyone can just go back to obsessing over their latest crushes and talking about new postings on YouTube. It's like it's up to me to remember Tom. If I let up, no one's going to pick up the slack. I can't imagine the whole world forgetting that a person exists.

On the way home, I let my sleuthing get the better of me. Every rustling leaf makes me stop to see if I can catch a glimpse of Tom's jacket. My eyes dart everywhere.

I even dare to swing by the Hanrahan house. Luckily, the truck isn't there and that gives me the courage to sneak into the backyard. Archie bolts toward me, tail wagging and tongue dangling as he reaches the end of his chain. Thankfully, he's not much of a barker. When I get within reach, he jumps up and bowls me over. Tom would've laughed hysterically and mocked me for being such a pushover. Archie frantically licks my face like I'm a soft-serve ice cream cone that's reached the critical dripping stage.

Call me morbid, but I have to check inside the doghouse for clothing fibers or traces of blood. I am relieved to find nothing more than clumps of dog hair and an old tennis ball. Noticing that Archie's water dish is empty, I refill it with the hose and set it back down beside the doghouse. Archie follows my every move—at least as far as his chain allows. I pat him and scratch his favorite spot behind his ears. Immediately, he drops, rolls over and awaits a tummy rub. As I oblige, I almost start to cry. Archie has never let me rub his belly, always scrambling up the minute I put my hand there when Tom had grown tired of the task. Clearly, Arch is longing for attention, and he isn't the least bit picky. After a couple of minutes, I get up, give the dog a hug, receive a final tongue bath and start for home.

I'm dejected by the time I head up our driveway and so consumed by trying to spot Tom, I forget to even act like I've been running. I'd walked the whole way home, not wanting to pass by anything too quickly. Seeing the Pathfinder in the driveway jerks me back to reality. It's time to face my dad for the first time since I'd confessed to my part in the affair that had whipped all of Richmond into a frenzy. I brace myself for another lecture, another proclamation of deep disappointment and, most likely, a few more conditions tacked onto my sentence.

Nineteen

Two days later, it's back to the school routine; another search mission will have to wait until next weekend. On the way to school, I'm stewing over the list of chores my father has posted on the fridge for me to do after school: mop the basement, scrub the mildew from the basement bathroom, do the laundry. Contrary to his speech about making my punishment meaningful, I figure it's all just a way for dear old Dad to get out of spring-cleaning and add an extra golf day to his week.

I am a couple of blocks from my house when Taryn McCloskey strolls out of her yard a few houses ahead. She stops at the sidewalk, looks my way and waits. Naturally, I peer back over my shoulder to see if someone else is behind me. There isn't anyone except for Patty Jervis's annoying, booger-eating little brother, Franklin, already enjoying an extra breakfast course. Taryn's still standing there, still looking toward me. Has being shut out of the "in" crowd made her stoop so low as to talk to me?

"Hi, Craig." Apparently it has. "Did you have a nice weekend?"

"Yeah." Not really, but "yeah" comes out. How many people actually admit their weekend sucked? As I walk, she walks too. Walking to school with Taryn McCloskey? I glance upward to see if Porky Pig is flying overhead. I know without a doubt that my face matches one of the reds in my sister's lipstick collection. "How was yours?"

"My what?" Taryn asks. Apparently, the weekend topic faded away during my thirty-second stupor. I don't bother to explain. I figure she will realize this is a big mistake and abruptly turn back with a lame excuse about forgetting something at home.

"Have you thought of an idea for your persuasive essay yet?" she asks. Okay. She is going to let this drag on.

"Not really." Of course I had. When you're stuck shining your father's stinky shoes all Sunday afternoon, you welcome the chance to think about schoolwork. "I thought of writing about why we shouldn't have to pay for field trips since we're supposed to get a free education."

"Wow. That sounds pretty serious." She is looking right at me without a bit of shyness or awkwardness. How come seventh-grade self-consciousness skips some people?

"I don't think I'll do it. I don't really know enough about it. Besides, I wouldn't want Miss Chang to cut out a day at Playland because of me."

"No. Everybody'd hate you."

How would I know the difference? "Have you picked a topic?"

"I'm going to write about ostracism. That's when people consciously decide to shut you out."

"Is that why you're walking with me?"

"Huh?"

Oops. I'd actually said that out loud. Now I have to explain. "Did you want to interview me or something? It's pretty obvious that I'm not exactly the most popular kid in class."

"Actually, I hadn't really thought about it. I never really thought you cared. Besides, it's not so much you as Tom. No offence, but he was ultra-obnoxious. Anyway, if you hadn't noticed, I'm not exactly with the 'in' crowd these days."

By now, it's clear that Taryn isn't going to bolt. Suddenly, I am comfortable around her. I guess when you say too much and the other person keeps talking to you, it kinda makes things safe. I plunge ahead. "I've noticed. Tracey and Erin have made it obvious that you're on the outs."

"Isn't it just so stupid?" Her voice gets a little higher. "They're being so immature. That's what I'm gonna write—ostracism is a cowardly way to deal with conflict."

"So, what happened?" I try to glance around discreetly. I am chatting with Taryn McCloskey. I want witnesses, but there is no one around but Franklin, and he is too focused on something on his finger.

"You mean between me and them?"

"Yeah. Why aren't they talking to you?"

"Oh, it's too stupid to go into." She stares straight ahead. I know it is time to pick something else to talk about—weather, hating tests, TV shows.

"It's about Kevin Conners, isn't it?"

Taryn stops in her tracks. For a moment, she even stops chewing her gum. "How'd you know?"

Please! Kevin Conners is in Mrs. Chappelle's class, and every girl acts as though he's the *only* guy that matters. All because of two dumb dimples. If you ask me, he is a total bore, but when did personality ever matter? "Just a guess," I answer.

The walk continues. "Wow. You're really observant. I never thought you paid any attention to anything."

"You think I'm stupid." Oops. Another keep-to-yourself comment. Maybe I'm just going for broke. It's not like Taryn and I are going to be BFFs so I don't need to be too careful.

"I don't know. To be honest, I guess last year I thought you were pretty dumb. Everyone thought so. I mean, you didn't ever do anything in Osmond's class. Now, though, you seem to know stuff."

"And that surprises you?"

"Sort of. I mean, it's hard to change an opinion you have of someone."

"Except when Kevin Conners is involved."

"Yeah. It's really stupid, eh? I can't wait to read my essay in class. I haven't started, but I've got a lot to say."

"Do you think it'll fix things?"

"Oh, who cares?" She spits the words out.

I can't wait to hear her essay too.

We finish the final block to school in silence, but for the first time I feel that someone else in grade seven matters. Someone else is actually above all the crap.

The morning walk was interesting, but things get truly bizarre after school. I can't say that I've ever had a twenty-year-old, muffler-challenged Chevy van with a Playboy bunny painted on the side waiting for me at school (or anywhere else) before. I know in an instant who the driver is, and I know there's a ninety-seven percent—make that ninety-nine percent—chance he's waiting for me.

I almost make a run for the back path, but I know I've been spotted, and I don't want to make matters worse. I take two more steps toward the road, and the driver gets out of the van, waves at me and leans on the side of the vehicle, watching my every move. No sense creating more of a scene than necessary.

He had waved, hadn't he? Waves aren't bad. I've never seen a gangster movie where the villain waves before shooting the unfortunate target between the eyes. Tom's brother is smiling—not a sinister smile, but more the kind you tentatively make in case corn is stuck between your front teeth.

"C'mere, Craig." Not like I have a choice.

"Hey, Jerry." I attempt to sound cool, but the two simple words come out as a showcase of my new three-octave range. I don't think either of us has ever addressed the other by name before. I'm surprised he even knows my name. Sure, we've seen each other many times at Tom's house, but he was about as interested in me as I am in my sister's friends. Even the couple of times when he watched a DVD with Tom and me, we talked to the screen, not each other. Maybe his dad drilled him on my name before sending him to finish me off.

"Ya seen Tom?" he asks, sounding as genuinely concerned as a guy can in three syllables. Maybe he isn't a henchman for his father after all.

"No."

"Yeah, well…me neither." He drops his head and shifts back and forth a bit. He looks like he is trying to keep himself together. Finally, he stares right at me and says, "You will. He'll come to you, I know it. Tell him not to come home, not that he would. Dad'll beat him to a pulp 'cuz he's pissed about the cops. They been nosing into his business. He's gettin' all worked up and says it's all Tom's fault. It's just like with Andy."

Andy, the long-lost oldest brother. Maybe he wasn't a murderer, but a murderee. Jerry continues, "He'll come to you 'cuz he trusts you. When he does, give him this."

Jerry pulls a plain white envelope from inside his jacket and passes it to me. "Don't open it. Just give it to him; he'll know what to do."

Without waiting for a response, Jerry turns, gets back in the van and starts it up again, drowning out all conversations within a two-block radius. He speeds off, leaving parents of first graders to scowl at me as if I were responsible for his driving habits and his choice of art. I stare down at the envelope, shove it in my pocket and wonder what the whole episode was about. I could open up the envelope, but I want to respect Jerry's wishes.

Twenty

"**Y**ou look like you've just seen a ghost." Leave it to my mom to pull out an over-worked expression and make it perfectly suit the occasion. My weird day had gotten weirder. They say things come in threes. First Taryn, then Jerry, and then Tom himself.

I realize that my mom has asked me a question of some sort and I haven't heard a word. "You must be tired, dear. I guess our argument with your sister last night must've kept you up. Why don't you go rest, and I'll fix your favorite dinner."

Mom has it programmed into her brain that Sloppy Joes are my fave just because I requested them two birth-days in a row—when I was four and five. Maybe she just likes to cling to those years, before my school grades dashed all her dreams of being the prime minister's mother. I'd rather have take-out Chinese or a DQ meal, but Sloppy Joes are still way better than broiled liver. I mumble, "Thanks," and retreat to my room.

I hadn't heard any arguing last night, but it must've been a big one if Mom is making special meals for me when I'm still grounded. Maybe if things are severe enough, she will lift my sentence. Anger isn't a big part of her personality. She can only be mad at one of us at a time. She's pretty much sunshine by nature. Maybe my sister had gotten a tattoo or quit school or something equally earth shattering on the Trilosky scale. Let her take care of the mildew in the bathroom. At any rate, I need some downtime to process Tom's visit.

It all began with the talking hedge. As I walked up the driveway after school, I must have been so preoccupied by what was in the envelope I'd received from Jerry that I was totally confused when I heard "Hey, Craig" and saw only the row of cedars separating our yard from the Carmichaels'. It wasn't as if I'd forgotten Tom's voice, but running into him in my own yard seemed far less likely than there being a talking hedge.

He popped out of the shrubs, and the first thing out of my mouth was, "You look like hell." Not a welcoming thing to say, but it was true. The familiar red jacket had several tears on the front and sleeves. His face was dirty, his hair was flat and greasy, and his eyes were like a zombie's. He was obviously exhausted.

"Have you been in a fight?" I asked.

"Worse. I'm not doing too well."

"No kidding." He continued to look blankly at me. We stood in the driveway without saying anything for at least a minute. I didn't know what to ask and I didn't know how much I really wanted him to tell me.

"Can we go in the backyard? I don't want to be seen."

"How about coming in? My parents aren't home."

"No. If I go in, I don't know if I'll be able to walk back out."

Tom sat on one of the back steps leading up to the deck, and I joined him. I kept taking peeks at the guy I'd assumed was either dead or hundreds of miles away. In a couple of weeks, it seemed like years had crept between us.

"How's school? You still goin' for bonus math?" Tom sort of smiled and quickly put his head down. He was trying to keep things light, but it fell flat. I took the cue though because the silence was too awkward.

"I haven't needed much help lately. I'm sorta getting it, believe it or not. Chang makes a point of calling on me all the time in class. I guess it's to keep tabs on me. The writing stuff is actually starting to—"

"Anyone talk about me?" There was a trace of urgency in Tom's voice.

"They talked for a couple of days, but not lately."

Tom stared at the railing. "Probably glad I'm gone. Can't blame 'em."

"Why'd you run off? What was gonna happen?"

"Look, I don't want to be a pest or anything, but have you got any food? I'm starving." He continued to gaze at the rail. I knew not to draw things out.

"Sure. Come in and I'll—"

"I'll just wait here." I went inside and looked for what I could take that wouldn't be missed. It was really creepy—like giving food you don't need or want to a canned food drive, except this time I knew the person who was getting it. When you can actually see a face, it makes donating canned kidney beans and cream of celery soup seem heartless.

I grabbed a grocery bag and filled it with some old utensils from the back of one of the drawers, the remaining third of a casserole from last night, several oranges, a box of cereal, lunch meat, bread and potato chips. I ran upstairs and grabbed soap, toothpaste and an unopened toothbrush. I stuffed everything in my old backpack, dished out the last two pieces of chocolate cake and brought it all outside.

"Here's some cake for starters."

"Thanks." Tom snatched the plate and began stuffing himself. It was a sad scene. I quietly slipped the fork I'd brought for him back in my pocket. Manners have no place when you're that hungry, I guess. With his mouth full of cake, Tom asked, "Have you seen Archie?" He stopped chewing for a second, waiting for my reply.

"I went by a couple of days ago and filled his water dish. He was friendlier than ever. I wanted to play with him, but I was afraid your dad would come home."

"I don't think anyone will have much to do with Arch now," Tom said. "He's really my dog even though he was s'posed to be Jerry's. I miss him—the dog, that is."

Jerry's name reminded me of my mission. The cake was gone, and it looked like Tom was going to get up and disappear again.

"Wait. You've got mail." I handed the envelope to him, and he shoved it inside his jacket.

"Thanks."

"Aren't you going to read it? It's from your brother."

"Later. I gotta go."

I followed him around front and watched as he pulled his bike out of the bushes. For a minute, I thought he was going to thank me for the stuff. "Good cake" was all he said. Then he added, "Make sure there's air in your tires. Maybe I can get back here and take you to my new home."

With that, he was off, leaving me with more questions than answers.

My bedroom door opens and Mom peeks in. "Dinner's ready—that is, if you still have room. I see you finished off the casserole and the cake. You need your own fully stocked refrigerator. Your father's going to have to get another promotion if we're ever going to get you through your teens."

Dinner is just Mom and me. Dad is at a business dinner and my sister is in solitary. When I ask about her, Mom just snaps, "Never mind your sister," and then quickly paints on a sugary smile and adds her standard, "Eat up. I don't want all this food to go to waste."

What a waste it is. Mom always seems to cook for six regardless of the fact that we are a four-person family who hardly ever eats together. There is enough meat for ten Sloppy Joes, not to mention the customary bowl of salad, steamed veggies and roasted potatoes. Thinking of Tom eating leftover casserole and cereal makes me feel sick. Now that I know he's within biking distance of our house, I'm more frustrated than when he was missing. It seems like things never go how they're supposed to when I'm around Tom. Why didn't I make him tell me where he was living? Why didn't I convince him to come inside so we could figure out some sort of plan to fix things? What if he never shows up again? I don't want to think that I could have made a difference when all I did was give him cake.

Funny, but when Tom showed up, I didn't feel any of my usual annoyance or the urge to shut him out of my life. Maybe all my mom's sunshine has soaked through my skin. He seemed so desperate and in need. When it comes right down to it, five years of history as friends is a whole lot more powerful than a few months of extreme irritation. I know I've let Tom down. He needed more from me. Too bad I still can't figure out how to help.

After little more than half a Sloppy Joe, I excuse myself, much to my mother's disapproval.

"That's why you shouldn't overdo it on snacks before dinner," she grouses. "A snack is just that. It's not supposed to be a buffet."

Twenty-one

Remember what I said about things coming in threes? I should be so lucky. Just before midnight, the string of strange events stretches to four. Our car alarm wakes me up. Then I remember we don't have a car alarm. Someone is sparring with our doorbell.

Dad either thinks I can sleep through anything, or he is too tired to censor himself because he mutters obscenities as he clomps down the hall. Mom follows, wide-eyed enough to advise him to peek through the peephole before opening the door.

Dad is too annoyed by the still-ringing doorbell and the drum accompaniment now being banged out on the door. He shoots off some more choice words, although at a lower volume. I am at the top of the stairs when he flings the door open.

"Gimme my son." Mr. Hanrahan doesn't really yell it, but there is a don't-mess-with-me force to his voice.

"And what would I want with your son?" Dad shoots back.

"Dear, don't aggravate him! He's probably drunk." Okay, that's what I'm thinking, but leave it to Mom to get it out in the open.

"I just want my son and then we can all get some sleep." Mr. Hanrahan half lowers his head in an attempt to look humble and/or gentlemanly. Strange what a desire to beat the crap out of your own kid will make you do.

"He's not here!" Dad tries to slam the door, but Mr. Hanrahan deflects it with his shoulder and pushes into the front hall. Mom jumps back but manages not to scream.

"Call the police, honey," Dad says.

"Police won't do a thing. My boy's been missin' for two weeks." Mr. Hanrahan scopes out every bit of the house he can scan from his position in the hallway. In the second his eyes sweep over me, I forget how to breathe. Good thing too. It's pretty hard to scream when you've got no air.

"Look, I can't help you. I don't know anything about where your son is."

"What's your kid know?"

He stares right at me, with only my Dad and four or five stairs between us. Dad doesn't make much of a barrier but eight sumo wrestlers and an RCMP blockade wouldn't be enough to reassure me.

Nothing happens for the next three-second hour. He holds his glare on me. "Where's Tom?"

"I don't know." To my surprise, I spit the words out. I am angry this man is in our house. I'm ready to defend not only Tom but my parents and even my sister.

"Have you seen him?"

"Not since they pulled him out of school." Normally, I'd never be able to lie so convincingly, but I vividly recall how Mr. Hanrahan reacted when Tom and I invented sandwiches in their kitchen. Some sort of survival gene has awakened from one of my little toes or my elbow. Tom needs to be protected from his father.

"The police are on their way," Mom breaks in.

Mr. Hanrahan calms a bit. "Good. It's about time they searched this place."

"What do you even want with Tom?" Oops. Way too much adrenaline in me. He easily dodges my father and leaps up the stairs. This time I think Mom shrieks, unless it is actually me, waiting to be beaten to death.

He glares at me with only inches between us. "He's my boy and I'll do what I want with him."

Dad grabs his shoulder, and Mr. Hanrahan turns for a moment to swat him away. Then he resumes trying to rip me apart with his eyes. I can't come up with any more words to spit out. Just saliva. Right on his nose. This time Mom does scream, just as the police arrive. Tom's dad grabs both my shoulders and shakes me as one officer somehow wedges his way between us and another shouts, "All right. Let's cool it." (Personally, I think a solid "Freeze!" and a swift handcuffing would have been perfect. Drag him out the door and push him to the ground.)

Mr. Hanrahan backs down the stairs, not even bothering to wipe his nose. "I'm just here to get my son." His voice holds a hint of despair.

As the police escort Tom's father out of the house, Mom acts as a human barricade to keep me from following. "You let your father and the police handle this. Now go back to bed." I am still angry and scared, my feelings too strong for sleep. I don't bother to argue though. When I am at the top of the stairs, my mother adds, "And no more spitting on people." It doesn't matter who is on our front lawn. Mom retains her position as chief-of-police, etiquette division, no contest.

Watching things die down from my bedroom window, I know my mother will be worried about what the neighbors think about the police coming to our house. It is a lot easier than thinking about what life must be like in the Hanrahan house.

Twenty-two

For the second morning in a row, Taryn and I walk to school together. We haven't made arrangements, but she is once again waiting on the sidewalk in front of her house. When she sees me and waves, I don't even do a shoulder check to see if anyone else is around. To be honest, I've been turning and scoping out what was behind me long before Taryn came into view. I am able to wave back casually without any risk of embarrassment.

The conversation sticks to yesterday's topic. For all her talk about not caring about what her fair-weather friends think, Taryn mentions them at least four times on the short walk to school.

As she rambles on about an incident last summer at Playland, I peer at the houses we pass and wonder where the new home is that Tom mentioned yesterday. It's a safe bet that I won't spot him in any of the front windows on my route to school. With the image of a worn and ragged Tom so clear in my mind, it is obvious that his home doesn't have food, running water or laundry facilities. I'm picturing something more like a *Survivor*-style fort made of twigs and branches.

I try hard to focus on Taryn's tragic tales of fickle friendship. I learn that you should never go in an odd-numbered group to an amusement park. Apparently the memory of sitting on a roller coaster beside a greasy-haired, acne-scarred stranger stays with you a long time.

"I have an apology to make," Taryn declares as she stops and looks at me. I stop and glance at her, but I can't sustain the gaze. It's too awkward.

"Do you remember that day in the gym when Tom beat you up?"

Come on, how do I forget something like that? Still, it's a sore spot to have Taryn refer to it as Tom beating me up. I was the socially responsible one. I stood there and took it. Not that I had a chance to do anything else.

I nod and, thankfully, she goes on. "Well, I think that was sort of my fault. That was back when I was in with Erin and the others. Anyway, Tom was bugging Erin. He like offered her this cookie that he'd half eaten. She said something like 'Gross' and he got all mad. He taunted her with stuff like, 'You know you want it. You know you like me.' I jumped in and said, 'Whatever. Leave Erin alone. Go find your boyfriend, Craig.' I didn't mean anything by it. I just wanted him to lay off. And then he took it out on you."

There you go. I guess Tom and I aren't the only grade-sevens with big confessions. When I dare to look at Taryn again, she has this pleading kind of look. I quickly say, "It's okay. You didn't know what he'd do."

"No. Exactly!" She sounds relieved as we walk in silence. I'm not the least bit mad—just disappointed. Yeah, Tom went berserk. Not that big of a surprise. I just wish he'd explained it himself. He got shot down by a girl. It was never about me at all.

After lunch Miss Chang tells us to work on our persuasive essays. I'm not all that committed to the field trip topic, so my mind starts to wander. Mr. Hanrahan's glare flashes into mind, then Tom's filthy face with chocolate cake crumbs in the corners of his mouth, then a close-up of my spit on Mr. Hanrahan's nose. Back in grade three, Tom and I used to have spitting contests to see who could spit the farthest. As with most things between us, it was never much of a contest. I was just pleased to get to the point where my spit no longer landed on my shoe. For his part, Tom eventually broke his one-meter record and raised his arms in Olympic-style glory. Tom would've high-fived me over last night's bull's-eye, even if it had come at close range.

"Why don't you have anything on your paper, Craig?" Miss Chang's one of those teachers who moves around the room instead of sitting at her desk, catching up on marking.

"I've got writer's block, I guess." There is at least some truth in that. Miss Chang crouches by my desk and quizzes me about my topic. She spends the next five minutes listening to my responses before recommending that I consider a different topic—something I feel passionate about. She expects an outline first thing in the morning. As if I don't have enough on my mind already!

Twenty-three

I rush home, hoping the cedars will talk again. Nothing. Maybe Tom is perched on the back steps. Nothing there either. I decide to go to the garage and check my bike in case Tom ever does reappear. Both tires are flat since I haven't ridden it in about four months. I pump the tires back up, give the bars a quick dusting and then head inside to try and figure out what I feel passionate about. Once again, nothing.

I zip down to the kitchen and scan the cupboards for something to snack on. We have masses of canned stuff, so I pull some down for Tom. I load six cans into a plastic bag, and there isn't a cream of celery soup among them. As I stuff the bag in my backpack, I go back to thinking about food drives and how poor people should receive both quantity and quality. Then I realize there is something that I'm passionate about. I run upstairs and, forgoing an outline, start to write. How commendable are donors who give up things that have little or no value to them? On the other hand, does a starving person care what's in the can? Shouldn't even the need-iest get to experience the small pleasure of eating some-thing truly tasty?

I fill three pages of notebook paper. My ideas rush out faster than I can get them all down. They aren't organized at all, but I know I can go back and do that on a rewrite. Wow. I'm actually planning to do another draft without any prodding. As I grab another sheet from my binder, I hear a *ping* on my bedroom window. I run to the window, peek out and see Tom searching the ground for another pebble to chuck.

Only a month ago, I dreaded seeing Tom. Now I'm both relieved and excited to see him again. I am probably his only contact, and I know I have to keep in touch with him until I can find a way to make his life less miser-able. There's this lump in my gut that tells me there's no way Tom can go home again unless Mr. Hanrahan gets thrown in jail for a decade or so. Tom needs a new start, and it's not going to happen as long as he has to keep hiding in the woods. For all my thinking that I'm a big shot at twelve, it's times like these when I know I'm still just a kid. How is it that one kid has to look out for another kid? As far as I can figure out, there aren't any other options. Grabbing my backpack and jacket, I head out.

"Is your bike ready or what?" No other words are exchanged. I pull my bike out of the garage and we are off. For a half-starved kid, he manages to set a wicked pace, faster than I am used to. I guess when your bike becomes an absolute necessity rather than a plaything there isn't time to idly zigzag down the street. If I hadn't been running regularly, I would never have been able to keep up. As it is, I am gasping when we hit a light. He doesn't seem out of breath at all.

We go along Number 3 Road past Steveston Highway. Tom and I have biked this area several times before. All housing developments end at Steveston, and there are empty fields, a few farms and then some business developments once you get closer to the water.

As soon as we veer left off the main road, I know where we are going—Finn Slough. I should have thought of that. We'd gone there only a few times, but it's the kind of quiet rundown place where a grimy scratched-up kid could go unnoticed.

Even though I've figured out our destination, it is still shocking when we pedal over the decrepit wooden bridge and pull up beside the beat-up fishing shack. This is the pathetic little hut that we once joked about giving one final shove so we could watch it slip and sink in the marshy drool of the Fraser River.

Tom leans his bike against the thicket of dead bushes and walks up to the open doorway. He turns, flashes a goofy, yet defiant, grin and says, "Welcome to my home. Get off your bike and come on in."

I feel nauseous, and I know it isn't because of the whirlwind pace we'd set getting here. I try to paint on the kind of smile you've got to drag out when your grandmother gives you a knitting kit for your birthday. Luckily, Tom turns away and ducks into the shack. I scan the building again and start to feel a deep sense of anger, combined with the nausea. Sure, we'd played inside the abandoned shed and we might have talked about camping out for a night, but that was in the summer when we both knew we had homes to return to after a little adventure. It was a cool place to hang, but it's no home. Rats deserve better. Even the victims of Tom's worst stunts wouldn't wish this on him.

What am I supposed to do? How can I act like everything is just swell? I need to shake someone— hard; I need to tell all the adults that this isn't supposed to happen to kids even if they've done a ton of stupid things. The whole scene screams, *Do something,* but I have no idea what to do.

I don't realize Tom has come back out again until he nudges my shoulder. "It's not so bad." His voice is soft and low. "Believe it or not, it's better than home, and it beats foster care. Just come in. It's really okay. I'm surviving."

I want to argue; anything has to be better than this, but I find myself unsuccessfully trying to fight back a couple of tears. For once, Tom doesn't make fun of me. He just yanks my jacket sleeve and guides me in.

Not so bad? Nothing could be worse. The scattered tires and nets should be decorating a landfill, not someone's home. An old chipped table is propped up against a wall with a bag of apples and the remains of my food donation on top. The opened doorways on both sides of the shack create a chilling breezeway.

How could a lousy squirrel stunt have led to this? Nothing makes any sense. I can't keep looking around the place. Ashamed and disgusted, I stare down at the floorboards.

"I really am doing okay." It's surreal. Tom is trying to comfort me when the roles should be reversed. I slump down to the floor, and we just sit there for a couple of minutes.

"You can't stay here. No matter what you say, this isn't living."

Tom stands up abruptly and walks over to the large opening overlooking the slough. When he turns back to face me, he looks angry rather than reassuring. His voice quakes as he speaks. "What am I supposed to do? This is all there is. I don't come from a perfect little family where my mom stays home and wonders what kind of cookies to bake. My mom just prays that all the bad stuff will go away. I don't have a dad that businessmen want to do lunch with. My dad goes off and bums beers at noon and then downs a pack of mints, hoping no one will notice the smell of booze when he goes back to work. I don't have a sister who wins trophies on the school track team and mulls over scholarship letters each night. My sister's been arrested four times for shoplifting and she spends all day in the basement smokin' pot. Jerry is the great hope. He almost made it through grade eleven, and he's got himself a job that he's kept for five months. He's a shining star.

"Haven't you figured out we're different? Don't you realize I got no chance? They can't shove me in foster care. They did that when I was in grade one, and I'm never going through that again. In eight months, I was tossed to three different homes. Seems I was a little too angry.

"There's a reason we've never talked much about my home life. If I told you even one story about it or about my foster home experiences, you'd pity me. I don't need that. But more than anything, I don't need you coming here and telling me that this—my life on my own in this shack —is unacceptable."

He is right. His big speech doesn't make me any less angry; instead, the anger kind of turns in at myself for being so stupid and so blind.

"Sorry."

"Don't go doin' that! I don't need you feeling guilty just 'cuz I'm pissed off about my life. Don't go feeling like you could've changed a thing. We're just kids. We can't fill out our own transfer papers and put ourselves up in Buckingham Palace. I never needed a friend to talk to about my family. I only needed someone to make me forget them for a while. I have to stay here for now, but I'm working on a plan. I'll be gone soon."

"To where?" Afraid to look Tom in the eye, I stare at the bag of apples. One of them has a bruise that covers most of the surface. I bet he'll eat the whole thing, bruise and all...maybe even core and all. "How will anything be any better?"

"Haven't you listened to anything I've said? I don't know that anything will be better. But at least it'll be different."

Tom sits on the floor and closes his eyes. I feel like I've stayed too long, even though only ten minutes have passed. He doesn't stir as I shuffle to my feet. For the first time, the weight of my backpack gets my attention—or my back and shoulders' attention, to be precise—and I remember I've come with housewarming gifts. I kneel down, unzip the pack and start unloading the food onto the table. After placing the fifth can, one of the table legs gives out, sending me chasing after a rolling can and two speedy apples that are in a race to escape from this dismal place. Tom continues to sit motionless. It is only as I start to walk out that he acknowledges me again. "I need you to get Archie."

"But—"

"I want Archie to come with me. You said yourself that no one's taking care of him and no one will. He's the only part of my past that I want to keep with me."

"Well, how am I supposed to get him?"

"Do I have to tell you everything?" he snaps. "Get him tonight. You'll only need to keep him a night or two tops.

I'll come get him Friday night or Saturday morning at the latest."

"Fine." And without hearing a thank-you or a good-bye, I walk out, wrestle my bike away from an overgrown bush and head home.

Twenty-four

At dinner, I poke at the lemon-herb chicken and vegetable medley that cover my plate and fill my mind with trivial questions. Why is it called a vegetable medley? Are my carrots going to sing some sort of oldie followed by a raise-the-roof showstopper by the Green Pea Choir? When will Mom ever get tired of lemon-herb chicken? Is this really what I deserve as a proper send-off before risking capture in the Hanrahans' yard by a man who is bound to remember how my saliva shellacked his nose? Why is my sister back at the dinner table? She's showing no gratitude for being released from solitary. Why are there little toadstools outlined in yellow on our paper napkins? Did Mom buy them for the pattern or were they marked down because toadstools have fallen out of fashion?

After my sister leaves the table and my mother begins her nightly counter-washing ritual, I continue to sit and stare at the three remaining peas on my plate. As long as I have a morsel to push around with my fork, I can delay facing possible death at the hands of Mr. Hanrahan. How demeaning that my last meal should include green peas! Then again, if Mr. Hanrahan does punch my guts out, I can be mildly satisfied knowing his face will be sprayed with green slime.

"What in the world are you doing, Craig?" My mother sounds irked. Not the kind of behavior you expect from a mom whose son is facing extermination in an hour or so. "Stop playing hockey with your food. I want to run the dishwasher." She unceremoniously snatches up the plate, swishes the little green guys down the garbage disposal and completes her urgent task.

Lacking any other ideas for a last-minute reprieve, I get up and grab my jacket. I turn to see my mother with a scoop of dishwashing powder in one hand; the other hand has found its familiar resting place on her hip. Her face tells me she is still thoroughly peeved. "And where do you think you're going? This is a school night. I'm sure you've got a lot of homework to do. You can't just walk out of—"

I exit mid-tirade. There will be a price to pay when I return, but I will be happy to face it if, in fact, I do return. Life in prison beats the death penalty. If I had let my mother finish, I could have stayed safe at home and blamed everything on parental authority, but I couldn't let down Tom, not to mention poor Archie.

Walking to the Hanrahans', I think about how my life has started to look up since Tom disappeared.

With all my training, I might do well in long distance running at the spring track meet. Taryn McCloskey has decided I am worthy enough to walk and talk with. I am on my way to getting a few grades above my standard C and C-minus this term. I've even earned a B and an A on a couple of writing assignments. But now I am off to face the scariest man I've ever met. There is a chance I can get in and out of the Hanrahans' yard undetected, but an expanding knot in my stomach tells me that won't likely be the case. It just goes to show you can never sit back and enjoy your own accomplishments, however slight they may be.

On the way over, my legs remain strong. Each stride is a normal span even though my mind urges me to take mini-steps. My knees bend as knees normally do and my calf muscles feel no tension whatsoever. Unfortunately, my upper half isn't nearly so composed. I've already gnawed down two fingernails; the third is a work in progress. My hands are shaky and my heartbeat matches the speed and sound of a jackhammer. My heart might very well leap out and go for the world's long jump record.

My thoughts would shame even the Cowardly Lion as I try to convince myself that dogs can live just fine tethered to a chain, day in and day out, starved of attention, food and water. I try to commend myself for off-loading leftovers on Tom. Plus I've served as a messenger between Jerry and Tom. I even spat in the face of the enemy. Surely, I've done enough, right?

But for all the "Don't do it"s and "Turn back now"s, a louder voice inside me—one that takes on Tom's tone and expression—shouts, "Do it, you wimp! Have some guts and do what you have to!" I wish the voice would shut up.

I walk down the back alley and edge toward the wooden fence that encloses the Hanrahans' backyard. If I can just sneak in and snatch Archie, everything will be fine. Despite all my worries of being caught and thrashed by Mr. Hanrahan, this should be an easy mission—steal family dog, run home, hand over dog, get on with life.

Faint lighting from the house on the other side of the alley helps me make out the gate. I pull the string to undo the latch, and nothing happens. Access denied. Someone has padlocked the gate. I can only get to Archie by passing through the carport at the front. Oh, why do I have to go with Plan B? So long to all calm, rational thought. My heart and mind start racing once again. I picture Mr. Hanrahan perched on the back steps, gun in hand, ready for a little target practice.

I wobble out of the lane and toward the front of the block, my lower half now as tense as my upper body. Lights are on in the house and, even worse, Mr. Hanrahan's truck is parked in the driveway. My lip starts to quiver. I am suddenly three and a half again, having stubbed my toe on the sidewalk, craving a hug followed up by some milk and cookies—Mommy's Medicine, she called it. I want Woofie, my ear-bitten childhood teddy. I think of simple pleasures like running through the sprinkler or licking the icing off the beaters while Mom bakes.

A distant siren snaps the toddler out of me. Great. The ambulance service is busy. If I take a bullet, I'll have to wait for medical attention. I start to whimper. If only I hadn't thought of the gun. Is it still at police headquarters? If so, wouldn't Mr. Hanrahan have pulled out an assortment of guns from the attic, ready for attack? What if he's given up guns and now sports a freshly sharpened machete?

Okay, the knife thing is over the top. The whole image of being slashed to death by a drunken maniac makes me turn and sprint for home. A block and a half into my getaway, I stop and turn back. I don't do it for Tom. No way. In my mind, I can hear him laughing at me for being a sissy. No, I do it for Archie—a starving, neglected animal that needs to be rescued. Like it or not, I am Archie's only hope. My nerves don't calm any, but I trudge forward.

The adrenaline starts bubbling, giving my legs a kick-start, and I am soon heading up the driveway and through the carport. The phrase *life or death* jumps into my mind, taunting me and distracting me so that I brush against the sideview mirror of the pickup. There's no escaping the reality that Mr. Hanrahan is home. I slog on. After turning to see no one seated on the back steps, I walk right up to the doghouse. Archie is fast asleep, lying on his side, head and forepaws spilling out of the doghouse. My quick approach causes him to jerk his head up and launch into a chorus of watchdog barks. Please, no! It's an alarm that no one on the block can ignore. Mid-heist, it's all or nothing. *Life or death.*

Archie pulls himself up and out of the shelter and lunges at me. Rather than pull back beyond the chain's reach, I quietly call Archie's name and he instantly goes from vicious beast to tongue-slathering pooch. His front paws rise in excitement to meet my shoulders. If I didn't have other things on my mind, I'd be more prepared, but I lose my footing, stumble to the ground and surrender once more to the saliva bath.

I look over my shoulder to see if all the commotion has caused a stir from the household. I see shadows behind the curtains, but no movement. I convince myself the shadows are furniture, not *him.* As I jerk my head to escape the tongue and the overwhelming gusts of dog breath, I roll out from under Archie, get to my knees and pet him as he frantically wags his tail and nudges his rear up against me. I wonder if he's had any attention since my last visit. Two empty bowls beside the doghouse affirm that I, Craig Trilosky, accomplice to the attempted murder of a squirrel and now neighborhood prowler and dognapper, am definitely performing an act of honor and—thoughts of Woofie notwithstanding—courage.

Although my head is telling me to unchain the dog and get out of here, I am a sucker for Archie's plea for a tummy rub. There he is on his back, impatiently snaking his body from side to side with legs bent. He tenses up for a second when I begin to scratch his belly and then lets out what I swear is a sigh as I move my fingers through his matted fur.

A hand on my shoulder abruptly closes the petting zoo. I freeze, fingers in mid-scratch, head rigidly tilted to the right—away from the intruding digits. Oh, God, this is it! *Life or...*I can't even finish the thought.

Twenty-five

I brace for a blow to the back of my head or a second hand closing around my neck. I am glad I can't see him. I'd rather have old Archie as my last vision than a close-up of Mr. Hanrahan's face.

"I figured you'd show up here at some point, Craig." My right ear eases off my right shoulder, my eyes pop back into their sockets, and I slowly turn to face Tom's mom. She smiles. Up until now, I didn't even know she had teeth. The hand on my shoulder, only moments ago a sign of imminent death, is now a source of comfort.

"Are you taking the dog?"

I nod.

"Well, you'd better hurry it up 'cuz my husband will be yelling for me any second. You don't want him seeing you here."

Okay…so comfort's a fleeting thing. I hustle to my feet and start to unhook Archie's chain.

"No!" If you can imagine a whispered yell, that's exactly how her voice sounds. She looks right in my eyes and continues, "If the whole chain's gone, he'll know somebody took him. He'll go straight to you. It needs to look like the dog broke away. I think there's an old leash under the steps."

She runs in that direction as I nervously pet Archie, who is now lying on his belly, obliviously licking his left paw. I glance back to the curtained living room window. My eyes zero in on a tall shadow. Is it a floor lamp? Or could it be Mr. Hanrahan, watching and waiting? Is the gun loaded? What's he waiting for? I quickly look away and my eyes dart back to Tom's mom. She is heading toward me with what looks more like a rope than a leash. She swiftly switches Archie's chain with the rope and hands the other end to me.

"Go. I'll tell him I must've left the front gate open and the neighbors saw the dog on the loose down the street. That'll keep him off you for a day at least. Go! And tell Tom I'm praying for him."

That's it. Archie and I are off, increasing our lead on all competitors. Maybe this is what all my training was really about. I don't need any gold medal or grand ceremony at the end. I am just relieved and surprised to be alive.

At the pace we're going, we could make it to my house in record time, but I don't have any say in which way we are going. Arch is alpha and I am definitely omega. Thanks to my eager guide dog, I tour a few blocks that I didn't even know existed. I guess *tour* isn't the word for it since

I have no time to sightsee. The immediate challenge is to move my legs in time with his. I fall once and, remarkably, Archie turns around to retrieve me. Out of breath, I slowly rise and try to get my bearings. The streetlights seem to morph into floodlights as they call attention to a pickup truck heading my way. As it nears, I know the game's over. I don't move. What's the point? I'm busted. I close my eyes. Just hit me and get it over with.

The truck races past. Archie nudges my leg, confused by the delay. We resume the race. Twenty minutes into the ride, Archie lets up enough for me to catch my breath, look around and steer us in the direction of home. Still, it isn't a straight path: Archie explores a few driveways and plows right through a mailbox. (Add a bruised hip to my med chart.)

Once we get to my driveway, it takes three tries before I can pull him up it. I guess when you don't know when your next walk will be, you prolong the one you're on as long as possible.

Thankfully, Mom isn't waiting at the top of the driveway, arms akimbo, lecture ready. Archie enters the garage without incident and inhales the crackers I scatter over some flattened boxes that I lay out as his temporary home. He laps at the pail of water and does a bunch of circles, clockwise and counterclockwise, before curling up for what I hope will be a quiet night's rest.

As soon as I have one foot in the house, Mom bounds into the kitchen, spouts off a variation of her standard, "Respect Your Parents" tirade and announces that time will be tacked onto my current sentence. The precise terms are to be decided, as always, "when your father gets home." I do my best to look remorseful, eyes fixed on a renegade pea that had rolled under the cabinet overhang. There is no point in putting up a defense as she rants about how disappointed she is. That will only rewind the speech to the beginning. With the best "I'm sorry" I can muster, I head to my room.

I shove my untouched math and science homework off the bed and, feeling very much like the squished bug (which I can't seem to locate on the ceiling), I close my eyes and drift off.

Twenty-six

A howling wolf awakens me at 1:26 in the morning. A wolf? In Richmond? Archie! The screaming in my left knee and whining in my right hip bring me to full alert. Why do a few hours of rest always make an injury feel worse? I hobble downstairs and manage to suppress the urge to mutter a few middle-of-the-night curse words I could say I learned from Dad.

When I get in the garage, Archie leaps at me, and I wisely lean against the garage door to prevent yet another fall. Ouch! I don't fall, but I am foolish enough to have positioned myself so the bruise on my hip receives the brunt of Archie's greeting. I collapse on Archie's bed, eyes fixed on the door, expecting it to open any second. As Archie follows me and sputters a few final woofs, I keep drawing blanks about how to explain what he is doing in our garage.

For some reason—maybe she's invested in some earplugs—Mom doesn't turn up, and I nod off. When I wake, hours have passed. Although it is a cold night, I am relatively warm since Archie has nudged his furry body against me. His snoring, rather than the chill, is what awakens me. Sleeping, Archie looks perfectly content. By curling up against me, he not only keeps warm but he also gets human attention. I'm not Tom, but I guess it isn't a time to get picky. Maybe he is also trying to thank me for all my efforts.

It is clear to me why Archie is such a must-have companion for Tom. For a moment, I wonder if I can keep Archie in the garage forever and tell Tom that I wasn't able to free Archie from the Hanrahan compound. Thou shalt not covet thy neighbor's dog, my conscience tells me, and I refocus on my mission of making Tom's hard up life more tolerable.

I peek out of the garage as the sky lightens. I have to hop back in bed before anyone catches me. All this sneaky stuff is hard to maintain. I'm a bit surprised Mr. Hanrahan hasn't paid us another visit, but I guess the police intervention from last time is enough to make him think better of accusing the Trilosky clan again. I look over to Archie. He's moved over slightly to take over my spot on the cardboard boxes. He's already sleeping again, his snore dulled just a little bit. I hope he can stay quiet for the day while I'm at school and then for one more night. I drift over and explain the plan to him as his eyes half open. If only he understood, he'd be sure to cooperate.

Being a Friday, Mom isn't around during the day. She has a Red Cross gig in the morning, followed by a

Meals on Wheels run. The afternoon might leave an hour or two open, but she mentioned something about some historical society that wants to save a tree or signpost or something. I cross my fingers that the big meeting is this afternoon. To be safe, I comment at breakfast about how they don't make trees or signposts like they used to. There, Mom, I'm behind you. Save the signposts!

When I go to school, my sleep-deprived body falls into my seat and my head bonds with the desktop. Although I am five minutes early, I don't have to make any effort to chat with classmates. Taryn hadn't shown up along the route to school, and I didn't dare knock on her door. As I'd approached the portable, I saw her on the steps with Erin and Tracey. They were happily yakking and giggling. Taryn didn't even acknowledge my "Excuse me" as I tried to step around them to get in the classroom. Inside, Keith and Mark exchange a flurry of comments in Chinese. Mindy has her head in what looks like a two-thousand-page book, give or take a few hundred pages. Despite all the dramatic flare-ups, the social rungs of seventh grade are always restored.

Miss Chang begins math four seconds after the final bell, and I struggle to raise my head off the desk as she asks Cam Stilwell for the answer to the first home-work question. I become more alert as I remember I've done only the first six questions of the thirty that were assigned. I have enough sense to get my hand up to answer questions two through six, but Miss Chang waits until number eight before calling on me. Busted! My school day will be extended half an hour, which wouldn't have mattered if Archie weren't hidden in the garage.

Recess and lunch pass without a single sign of recognition from Taryn. Apparently, she is too busy basking in her return to popularity. I spend the last half of lunch at my desk rewriting my persuasive essay. I even use a dictionary to check a couple of words.

Ten minutes into our writing period, I shock Miss Chang by presenting a completed second draft. She underlines several words as she wades through it and grins widely when she comes to the end. To be honest, I'm not even mildly surprised by her reaction. I feel strongly about my topic and am proud of how I've argued my points. Her only criticism—hey, teachers have to throw in some pointers or they'll be out of a job—is I need to use a thesaurus to punch up the words she's underlined. A thesaurus! A year ago, I'd struggled with where a simple period went and now I've leapfrogged ahead to using a thesaurus. If teachers got paid for their successes, Miss Chang would be moving into a mansion by June.

Twenty-seven

I fit in an extra run after school, not by choice but due to the fact that I am late and I want to beat Mom home before she discovers Archie. I am sore from yesterday's injuries and stiff from sitting at a desk all day, but I cope pretty well after the first couple of minutes.

Thankfully, the driveway is empty as I sprint to the finish line. Without a cool-down, I go straight for the garage. I know Archie will pounce on me as soon as I open the door, so I swiftly slip in and lean against the wall.

Once again, the dog takes me by surprise. It isn't his leaping or his licking or his barking. It is his complete lack of reaction. I scan the garage to see if he's curled up behind a crate or under my dad's workbench. Cold sweat oozes from my armpits and trickles down my forehead as my survey turns up nothing. Archie is gone.

Trying not to panic, I wonder if Tom has jimmied the lock and broken in to get his dog a day early.

My sweat glands go into overdrive as Mr. Hanrahan appears on my suspect list. If he has taken Archie, surely he'll be back to pulverize me until I spit out Tom's whereabouts. Even then, he might decide to finish me off just for fun.

"Looking for the dog?" Okay, I scream like a girl. Having totally spooked myself, Mom's surprise entrance puts me over the edge. "Your friend's dog needs leash training," she adds as I try to pull my heart down from the ceiling.

"Did you take him back?" I sputter.

"Oh, no. That's your job. He's in the car. I just drove him to McDonald Beach and tried to take him for a walk."

Strangely, there is no mud on Mom's pants. No rips or tears. No facial scratches. But there is no time to dwell on her apparent mastery of doggy discipline. I am stuck on the "job" she's assigned me. To the rest of the world, my mom is Florence Nightingale. But now she is asking for front row tickets to her only son's execution.

"Do you know whose dog he is?" I ask, setting the stage to begin some serious begging.

"Of course I do. And there's no way we can keep him. I don't want that man coming anywhere near our house again."

"Then you know I can't return him. Don't you remember how demented Tom's dad is? I spit in his face, Mom. He'll beat me beyond recognition. I only need to keep Archie here until the morning."

"Absolutely not! I'll drive you and the dog back as soon as I check to see if your father has phoned." She leaves the garage, and I desperately try to come up with a way to convince my mom that returning Archie is totally out of the question. I can't think. Panic has overpowered my brain cells. I crouch down and bury my head in Archie's fur.

Mom is back in no time. She stands in the doorway, hands on her hips, looking mighty peeved. I go back to hugging Archie. She'll have to drag us both to the car.

"Come," she calls. Archie tugs away from me and bounds over to her. The dog doesn't know she's against us. "Craig, get up. I don't have time for this nonsense. I'll be in the car the whole time. Everything will be fine."

"Do you really believe that?" I yell. Okay, it's not the best way to begin a negotiation, but my frustration and fear are raw. "Returning Archie to the Hanrahans would be the biggest mistake ever. No one cares about him. Can't you see how much he craves a little attention?"

"Craig, I can't go around protecting every animal that needs a better home."

"Why not? That's what you do. You help everyone. Right now, Archie needs us."

"I don't break the law, son. And I'm not about to start."

I break down. I spill everything I know about Tom and the Hanrahans. Although I know Tom would be furious, I mention his past stint in foster care, Jerry's warning that Tom can't go back home and even the time when I saw Mr. Hanrahan go after Tom. I spare no details. This time it's my mom who sits on the floor and hugs Archie. I talk about how much Tom needs Archie. I describe how pathetic things looked when I visited Archie last weekend.

Mom wipes away a few tears of her own, but I go on. "Don't you see? Tom stood up for me. When he took all the blame for the squirrel incident, his life completely changed. Me, I'm grounded, but he's got nothing. No home, no family, no food, nothing. Archie belongs to him. Tom deserves that much. If I hadn't gone with Tom to the park that day, none of this would've happened."

Mom breaks. She starts to cry and comes over to hug me. We're both a complete mess. Archie senses the urgency and gets in the group hug. "This isn't your fault," my mother says through her sobs. "Sometimes it's not a matter of *if* something is going to happen, but *when*. That incident was just the tipping point."

"I have to do what I can to make things right," I plead.

She hugs me harder and whispers, "Okay."

Neither of us has the energy to say anything else.

Twenty-eight

My mom has proven to people of all ages, abilities and income levels that she is a caring soul, but I hadn't seen how well she can talk to the animals until Archie came along. Maybe she's always been careful not to fawn all over people's pets so my precious sister won't feel guilty about her allergies, and I won't start pressing for a pet of my own.

With Archie, she finally lets down her guard. Mom hauls in a space heater to warm up the garage, followed by an old beanbag chair from the basement so I can be more comfortable. She even serves my dinner (an attempt at turkey sausage lasagna I hope she doesn't try again) in the garage and brings a couple of cooked burgers for Archie. If she hadn't stayed to pat and hug Archie as he gobbled down the patties, I would have gladly traded meals with him.

A short while later, she barges in with a box of dog treats. She sits on the concrete, marveling time and time again how well the pooch can shake a paw, lie down and, to her greatest amusement, play dead.

In the middle of Archie's eleventh or twelfth command performance of *playing* dead, we hear the *walking* dead come moaning and grunting up the driveway. Before Mom can finish her standard "Good heavens!", I'm out the door and staring at what looks like an extra from a horror movie. While I stand there gawking like an idiot, Mom runs directly to the shivering, soaking wet figure and rushes to get Tom into the house. Mom's body engulfs Tom's as they shuffle to the front door. As awkward as it looks, they move at a pace that would overtake the average high school track star. Tom doesn't speak; I'm not sure he is able to.

"CRAIG! THE DOOR!" Her words knock me out of my stupor. I run past them and push the door open, allowing them to hobble into the living room without even a moment's setback.

The next five minutes is a flurry of activity that would be the envy of every emergency room in the country. Doctor Mom barks out orders as I scramble to keep pace: "GET BLANKETS!" Stat! "GRAB SOME OF YOUR CLOTHES!" Stat! "GET THE THERMOMETER FROM THE MEDICINE CABINET!" Stat! "BOIL SOME WATER!" Stat! "RUN ACROSS THE STREET AND GET DR. KALMUS. TELL HIM IT'S PROBABLY HYPOTHERMIA!" Stat!

When my mom talks to Tom, she speaks in a gentle whisper as she quizzes him about his name, age and the date; he mutters incomprehensible syllables in reply. By the time I return with our neighbor, Dr. Kalmus, Tom is shrouded in layers of blankets while Mom holds a mug to his mouth and forces sips of hot tea through his whitish blue lips. Feeling totally useless, I attend to Tom's bike, which has been abandoned in the middle of the driveway. I prop it against the back steps, out of sight from passersby.

When I return to gaze at the medical unit in motion, my mother directs me to bring Archie in to see Tom. Somehow I'd managed to tune out the dog's persistent barking.

Archie bolts from the garage and begins making wide circling sweeps of our front lawn, frantically sniffing the ground and looking for his owner. Barking becomes high-pitched whimpering. I can't catch him as he zigzags every which way. Calling his name proves useless. All I can do is stand and wait. Finally convinced that Tom is not outside, Archie stops, looks up at me and trots to the door. As I open the door, I block Archie's entry, afraid that the dog will pounce on Tom and hurt him. I grab the fur on the back of his neck and attempt to guide him slowly to the living room.

That works for a millisecond. One sniff, and Arch is out of my grasp, darting to the sofa. Mom looks as if she is about to scream at me but, remarkably, the dog slows on approach, seeming to sense his master's fragile condition. He gently nudges the blankets that warm Tom's legs, all excitement shifting to his tail, which swiftly sweeps the air. Tom's face, smooshed against a back pillow, attempts a smile, an action that appears to cause intense discomfort. The rest of his body lies motionless as he tries to say the dog's name. "Arrrr" is enough to cause the dog to lean a little more into Tom's body.

"You're doing fine, Tom," Dr. Kalmus declares as he inserts a thermometer between Tom's lips. "Let's just see how quickly you're warming up."

"I think he's getting some color in his cheeks," my mom comments. Dr. Kalmus makes a humming noise and nods his head ever so slightly as he peeks at his watch before removing the thermometer.

"Yep. You're already up point five. That's good news, Tom. A degree or two colder and we'd have had to cart you off to the hospital. You're in good hands here." Dr. Kalmus smiles and gives a quiet chuckle as if to show there is nothing to worry about. He rises from the sofa to put on his coat. As he heads to the door, he mumbles a few directions to my mother. She thanks him profusely; the doctor deflects all praise, saying, "Heck, I gotta do something to earn your special Christmas baking, Kate." He chuckles again and is on his way.

I continue to stand about eight feet from the couch. As my mother goes back to tending to Tom, I feel utterly useless. Each time I glance at Tom, I feel I am gawking, so I gaze at the family portraits on our mantel until I feel guilty for having a family that is relatively normal.

My eyes look down and zoom in on a small carpet stain that is a faint remnant of a grape Popsicle mishap from last August. My mom startles me as she touches my shoulder and says, "He'll be fine. Maybe some painful blisters from the cold, but nothing more. Now go call your sister at Theresa Abagon's house and see if she can spend the night there. The number's on the fridge. This dog's staying in tonight."

In the morning, Tom is up and ready to return to life as a fugitive. Mom forestalls all that, insisting that he park himself at our kitchen table as she loads and reloads his plate with homemade waffles, each round featuring a different topping. Tom offers no resistance after his first bite. Archie curls up on Tom's feet underneath the table. Nobody protests when Tom's half a waffle "accidentally" slides off his plate to the floor.

Tom and I exchange a few grunts which pass for conversation until my mother excuses herself from the room. After a great deal of prodding, Tom provides a sketchy account of how he came to be wet and half frozen. Apparently, a police officer had parked at Finn Slough and started searching the grounds, shining his flashlight in all directions. Tom figured the guy was looking for him, so he panicked and took off on his bike. On the shack side of the slough, the path dead-ends at the river's edge. He figured it was the only place to hide so he waded in, bike and all, and did his best to stay submerged. A couple of flashes of light stretched to the water's edge, but not beyond. No one goes for a swim in the Fraser River in winter, right? Tom stayed in the water till he thought things were clear. It didn't make much sense to me, but he took offense at my follow-up questions, and the talk was over. All I know is he biked to our place after that, because he thought he would freeze to death.

I haven't thanked my mom for her miraculous, take-charge action plan, and no doubt within twenty-four hours, her superhero costume will be back in mothballs and she'll be nagging me about the clutter on my desk, the hazards of being a couch potato and the fact that I should be reading something to help my mind grow. Even so, I'm proud she's my mother. Sometimes you have to be aware of the alternatives to really appreciate how good you've got it.

Twenty-nine

According to Tom's original plan, he and Archie were supposed to be long gone from Richmond after breakfast. He planned to meet Jerry at his brother's job site at the crack of dawn. But that was before the Polar Bear Swim in the Fraser River. Mom has grounded all departures. She made an early morning trip to the meeting spot and informed Jerry that all plans had to be delayed. Jerry protested, but Mom stood her ground. Tom needed at least twenty-four hours of imposed rest.

After the waffle binge, Tom sleeps on the sofa for the rest of the morning and well into the afternoon. Maybe sleep is part of how you recover from hypothermia, but I think all Tom's time in a shack without heat, doors or proper meals has finally caught up with him. Archie makes his way onto the sofa, blanketing Tom's legs and feet.

It's kind of a drag having someone asleep in your living room. I never realized how often I pass through it to get somewhere else in the house. At first, I try tiptoeing, but as Tom's snores rise to a roar, I abandon any attempt at courtesy. I could crank the TV and the stereo, and it wouldn't make any difference.

When Mom returns from doing errands, she is toting a couple of bags from the mall. Must've been another sale on shoes. As she pulls out a guy's jacket, I start to complain. I hate when she tries to pick out my clothes!

"It's not for you," she snaps. "You've got plenty. That friend of yours can't go off to Moose Jaw with the one he's got."

"Moose Jaw? He's going to Moose Jaw?"

"Well, yes. Didn't he tell you? What in the world do you two talk about?"

Funny. Not long ago, she had forbidden me to talk to Tom. Now she seems to think we aren't talking enough.

She pulls a couple of packages of underwear, some socks and a sweatshirt out of the other bag. Ick. Who wants your friend's mother buying you underwear? I know Tom won't have the tact to pretend to be grateful.

"Why's he going to Alberta?"

"Moose Jaw's in Saskatchewan, Craig! You see, this is why geography still needs to be a subject in school. I'm going to have a talk with your principal when I'm in next week." Maybe Mrs. Brewer will lose her cool and tell Mom it's me, not the school, that's lacking. "Now go to the car," she directs as she unpackages items and cuts off tags. "There's a couple more bags."

Well, this is something—Mom's do-good nature being played out in our own home. On Tom, no less! Getting directly involved in the rescue effort seems to have thawed the icy relationship that had been building over the years. Clearly, Mom's in her glory, putting all that field experience as a volunteer into action.

We move to the den when Tom wakes up. Tom holds the remote in his right hand as he flips from channel to channel. He seems to be soaking in as much TV time as possible. Nothing has changed on the tube, but Tom has to figure that out for himself. His left hand repeatedly visits a plate of homemade double-fudge cookies. The bowl of grapes is just decoration. Mom never gives up.

"So what was in the envelope from Jerry?"

"Huh?" Tom is so engrossed in the TV screen, I think he forgets I am in the room.

"The envelope from Jerry—what was that about?"

"Money. He gave me cash to buy a bus ticket to go to Moose Jaw, but Archie can't go on the bus. I spent it on food. Man, was he pissed about that!"

All of a sudden, Tom drops the remote and leans forward. "Nuggets and Mavericks! How'd I miss this? Haven't seen a game since—well, you know." It isn't much of a game. The Mavericks are way ahead. I shut up and watch.

As the ref confers with the time-clock guy, Tom says, "Can you believe I haven't played basketball since

I took off? I actually forgot about it for a while. How weird is that? They better have a good basketball team in Moose Jaw. I hope it's not all hockey."

"So you've seen Jerry?"

"Yeah. Biked up to where he works and told him to come up with a new plan. He's got a couple of days off, so he and his girlfriend are driving me there."

"Okay, so what's with Moose Jaw?"

"Lame, eh? My uncle's there. He saw me when I was, like, two, but I don't remember him. Hope he's cool. He hates my dad, so I guess that's something."

"Is he your dad's brother?"

"No way, man! My mom arranged everything. Jerry says she made the calls from church so Dad wouldn't figure things out."

Back at Finn Slough, Tom had said I didn't know anything about his family. He was right. I guess I didn't ever want to know much. Moving to a place named after an animal's mouth doesn't sound very exciting, but maybe that is the point.

With the game resuming, Tom focuses on the screen again, and I start to think about how things are going to change. It's easy to get nostalgic when you know a big change is in the works. I remember how cool Tom thought he was when the grade-seven basketball coach let Tom hang out for after-school practices three years ago. As a tag-along, I was allowed to warm the bench, but Tom got to set up drills and even participate occasionally when they were a man short. His ego got unbearable until Casey Tisdall, the team's hotshot, pretty much skunked him in a game of 21 after one of the practices. I can admit now that I was cheering for Casey.

Tom starts yelling at the TV. He's ticked that the Mavericks are starting to let up and coasting to the win.

I think about the afternoon we shot free throws for five hours straight. I was proud to hit a streak of eleven in a row, but Tom broke thirty...twice!

I'm sure I'll get rusty on my free throws once Tom's gone. It's weird. This was the year Tom was supposed to be the star player on the team, and now that dream's dead. Like Tom, I hope there's some sort of program in Moose Jaw. If there isn't, I bet Tom will do something about it. I can't imagine him giving up basketball.

I know I began the year wishing I could break away from Tom. Well, that's a done deal. There's a lot I won't miss. I've had my fill of trips to see the vice principal. I took a lot of foolish risks with Tom egging me on. And some of Tom's taunting was just plain cruel. But no one has ever made me laugh as hard. Tom has a knack for getting me to loosen up and just be a kid. Maybe that's what people mean when they say, "Be careful what you wish for."

I wonder if I'll have any luck in making friends with someone else at school. Even though this is my sixth year there, I don't know much about my classmates. The problem is I don't know how to change that. Maybe I'll have to wait and start over in high school. In a twisted sort of way, Tom may have outdone me one last time. At least his new start begins tomorrow.

That kind of thinking gets depressing, so I shake it off and do my best to get into the game. Mavericks up by fourteen with a couple of minutes to go. Not a nail-biter, but good enough as a distraction.

Thirty

Just after midnight, Tom barges in my room and yanks the pillow out from under my head. "Dude, get up! I can't sleep."

He turns on the light, and, with no pillow to cover my eyes, I pull up the sheets. Another swift yank and the covers are on the floor.

"Come on!" I complain. "We gotta get up at five to get you to your brother's work."

"Yeah, so? It's a long drive. I can sleep in the car. Get up! I'm telling you I can't sleep. The sofa's cool and all, but I'm starting to worry about my uncle and where I'm going. Let's play some basketball."

I let out a loud sigh and sit up. "You can't play. If someone sees us, they might report you."

"So we won't dribble. You suck at it anyway. Just Twenty-One. Don't let the ball bounce. We don't even need a light."

"You're crazy!" I say as I get out of bed. I pull on a sweatshirt, and we are outside in less than a minute.

Archie pokes around in the hedges before sitting on the driveway and watching us.

Tom stands staring at me. "Uh, stupid, it's bad enough that we're not playing a pickup game, but I'm not gonna pretend with an imaginary ball. Where is it?"

Hmm, good question. We always played with Tom's. Something about it being an "official NBA ball." After about five minutes of snooping around the garage, I find it in a plastic tub with a bunch of other forgotten stuff like a bocce-ball set, a football and a Super Soaker.

When I reappear, Tom shouts, "About time. Game on!"

"Shut up. You'll wake my mom up."

"Yeah, you shut up." He grabs the ball from me and passes it back and forth between his hands. "She's okay. Can't believe she bought me undies, but that's cool. Need 'em."

"Hey, no dribbling!" No surprise Tom can't seem to control himself. I am going to have to be referee and player.

"So, it's Twenty-One, right?" I say, wanting to get on with things. "I'm only playing one game and then I'm going back to sleep."

"Yeah, yeah. One game. I haven't played in weeks, but you go first. You need every break you can get."

I haven't played in weeks either, but whatever. I figure once I take the first shot, Tom will get in game mode and shut up.

I can see well enough from the streetlight as I mentally line up my shot. Aim and miss.

"You suck!" Okay, so I've forgotten. Game mode comes with more talk.

His first four shots go in. So much for being out of practice. By the time he is up 16–4, I am tired of his putdowns on my every miss. When it is my turn again, I look toward the net and then chuck the ball at Tom's head. I miss that too.

"Hey! What's with you? That is so not cool! Show some sportsmanship, dude."

"Sportsmanship? You're telling me about sportsmanship? You say 'You suck' or 'Girl power' every time I miss and then there's 'Whoosh' and 'So pro' whenever you get one in, and you wanna tell me about sportsmanship?!"

It is time for me to go back to bed, and I march to the door. I have every right to forfeit the game, guilt-free. Tom runs in front of me and blocks my way. "Come on, man. I was just being funny. Let's just play. I'll lay off, I swear." He has a weird, pleading look in his eyes. One game; his last night in Richmond. I cave.

We play at least twenty games. I even win a couple. And, yeah, I throw the "You suck" stuff right back at him. So much for taking the high road. At 3:30, we finally turn in. It is a classic Tom occasion—incredibly annoying, but beneath it all, still fun enough to keep it going.

Two hours later, another visitor tries to kick me out of bed. Mom is easier to ignore than Tom. She goes off in a huff, and a minute or two later a wet tongue drowns out any chance of another dream. Tom howls as I squirm to pull away from Archie.

"Best dog ever, eh?" he says. "Come on! We gotta get going. If we're not in the parking lot by six, Jerry might change his mind."

It takes five minutes to throw on some clothes, hit the washroom and get in the car. I figure anyone else dumb enough to be up this early on the weekend won't care what I look like.

Once Tom loads his bike in the back, we are good to go. Archie seems to sense something is up, and he darts from window to window in the car until my mom orders Tom to grab hold of him. Mom's serious about her driving. We suffer through a Norah Jones CD that I am beginning to think might be stuck in the car's CD player. I am too tired to react, but when Archie frantically starts licking as Tom pretends to choke himself, I burst out laughing.

"Everything okay back there?" Leave it to Mom to think a little laughter might be a problem. Tom reads my mind, and we both laugh even more.

Jerry's van is the only vehicle in the parking lot when we pull up. His girlfriend has her head up against the window of the passenger seat, and Jerry stands by the storefront, smoking a cigarette and shaking from the morning chill. He hollers, "Hurry up" as we open the doors.

I grab the suitcase Mom has dug out from our attic and Tom retrieves his bike. Mom pats Archie and coos a bunch of nonsense in his ear.

With everything loaded, Tom tugs on the leash, and Mom lets go of Archie. "Oh, Craig," she calls, "did you give him your email address?" The stunned look on my face is signal enough for her to go digging in the Pathfinder for a pen and paper. She jots my email, our address and phone number on the back of a receipt, hands it to me and shoves me forward.

Jerry is in the van and has the engine running. "Here," I say as I hand Tom the paper. *Keep in touch* would've sounded lame.

Tom looks at me for a second and says, "Thanks." For the paper, maybe for more. I can't be sure. As he steps into the van, he adds, "I'll be in the NBA, you know. I'll get you free tickets one day."

I nod and wave as the van pulls out of the parking lot. Tom is moving on, and so am I.

Thirty-one

At school the next day, it's time to read our essays in front of the class. After seeing Tom off and getting a bit of a nap, I'd spent a couple more hours on mine. I even read it to my mom and punched up a few parts based on her suggestions.

Roger Battersby volunteers to go first. It's obvious he's just looking to get it over with. He's ghostly white as he stands before the class. He clenches his paper tightly, raising it up as some sort of protective shield. I don't have a clue what his speech is about. He reads it in a speed-mumble. Twice Miss Chang asks him to speak up, but then she too gives up.

More speeches follow. Mark Tam goes for the heart-strings as he talks about his memories of learning a card game from his now deceased grandfather. Cam Stilwell takes a safe route as he aims to convince us that hockey should be Canada's official sport. (Isn't it already?) Taryn takes her place up front and speaks without any notes. As I listen I'm disappointed, but not surprised.

She's abandoned ostracism and instead gives a cutesy talk she calls "The Price of a Smile." Yeah, it's predictable. In the end, she says a smile is—get ready for it—priceless. People clap; I groan.

Finally, it's my turn. Before beginning, I glance at my audience. Miss Chang offers an encouraging nod. Mark looks intense, like he's going to be graded on my speech. Mostly though, my peers seem distracted, burned out from the succession of speeches. Strangely, this annoys me. I want to be heard.

I look down at my paper and pause to make a silent dedication. And then I start.

I've been thinking a lot about cream of celery soup lately. Not craving it. Does anyone? Just thinking about it.

My voice is a bit scratchy, probably from saying nothing for the past hour. I clear my throat and continue. No more snags. The words pour out. I have purpose, I have passion.

Cream of celery soup. Ever had it? Sludge in a bowl. A soup whose star ingredient is the symbol of blandness: celery. Stare at a stalk. Even the color lacks impact: watered-down green. And somehow when they mush it up in a blender, it comes out pukey beige.

We've had canned food drives every year I've been at school. "Let's fill the classroom box! Maybe this year we can overwhelm Miss Newman's car. Maybe it'll take a van. No candy bars, please." (We don't want needy people having any treats now, do we?) Make it healthy foods, non-perishable…and bring lots.

Cream of celery. Healthy? I suppose. Non-perishable? Check. Lots? Double check. Triple and quadruple check! We have a whole shelf at home in one of the lower kitchen cupboards that is devoted exclusively to cream of celery. Cheap soup, bought on sale, no less. Oh, what a success for each and every food drive!

Why does no one ever talk about good taste? Are we so cold that we really believe that "beggars can't be choosers"? To donate phlegm in a can is just plain wrong. When we go for cheap and tasteless, we basically put a lesser value on the life of the recipient. We don't eat it, so why should they? Acts of charity should make a difference, not highlight a difference.

Have you ever been alone? Completely alone? You and no one. You and nothing. Homeless. I'd like to think that I'll never face that possibility, but who's to say? We've all seen homeless people. Each one has a unique story about how he or she got to the point of living in a shelter or outside a bank on a couple of ragged blankets discovered on garbage day or in a shack that even the rats have abandoned. Does it really matter how people got there? Why does the street person with a dog by her side get more coins from passersby than the homeless man who talks to himself? Without knowing their life stories, how can we be so quick to judge?

Perhaps what we all need is an opportunity to meet and understand a person who is down and out. As well as food, clothing, shelter and skills, maybe we need to offer hope. If you get to the point where you are truly alone, all the strength inside you may have been sucked dry, and maybe it takes encouragement and inspiration from others to offer hope that things will get better.

That inspiration has to come from something more than a can of cream of celery soup.

I fold my paper in half to signal that I'm done. There is awkward silence. Did I bore everyone into a stupor? Maybe I should've said, "The End," like a half dozen of my classmates. The pause has been too long for that now. I shoot a pleading look at Miss Chang, who starts to applaud. Is she beaming? Others join in. It sounds loud. It feels great.

I return to my desk and Jenny Tai whispers a simple, "Wow!" Mark gives me a thumbs-up. Others continue to clap and smile. I am able to smile back with confidence. Maybe Taryn was right about the whole smiling thing.

When we're dismissed for recess, Miss Chang asks me to stay behind. As I walk toward her, I don't feel any pang of dread, and I don't recap my morning for possible offences. It's all good.

"I'm just blown away, Craig," she gushes.

"Thanks." I grin broadly and add, "It felt a bit weird when everyone got so quiet at the end."

"You had them, Craig. When you began with the soup, all doodling, all whispers, all daydreaming stopped.

And that silence at the end? We needed time to let your message sink in. You made them—and me—think. All I can say is thank you."

The grade? I told Miss Chang not to tell me. After all, I didn't do it for a grade or for my teacher. I did it for myself. And I did it for Tom.